Lernkrimi Englisch

SHOTS IN THE MIST

Sieger im 2. Krimi-Schreibwettbewerb

Barry Hamilton
Nach einer Idee von Maria Gebhardt

Compact Verlag

Bisher sind in dieser Reihe erschienen:
- Englisch, Französisch, Italienisch, Spanisch: B1, B2
- Englisch GB/US, Business English: B1, B2
- Deutsch: B1
- Sammelband Lernkrimi Englisch, Spanisch: B1/B2

In der Reihe Compact Lernkrimi Kurzkrimis sind erschienen:
- Englisch, Französisch, Italienisch, Spanisch, Deutsch: A2

In der Reihe Compact Lernkrimi History sind erschienen:
- Englisch: B1, B2, Italienisch: B1

In der Reihe Compact Lernthriller sind erschienen:
- Englisch: B1, B2, Spanisch: B1

In der Reihe Compact Lernstory Mystery sind erschienen:
- Englisch: B1, B2

In der Reihe Compact Lernkrimi Hörbuch sind erschienen:
- Englisch: B1, B2, Business English: B2
- Französisch, Italienisch, Spanisch: B1

In der Reihe Compact Lernkrimi Audio-Learning sind erschienen:
- Englisch: A2, B1

In der Reihe Compact Lernkrimi Sprachkurs sind erschienen:
- Englisch: A1/A2

Lernziele:
- Grundwortschatz, Grammatik (A2, B1)
- Aufbauwortschatz, Konversation (B2)

In der Reihe Compact Schüler-Lernkrimi sind erschienen:
- Englisch, Französisch, Spanisch, Latein, Deutsch, Mathematik, Physik, Chemie

Weitere Titel sind in Vorbereitung.

Chefredaktion: Dr. Angela Sendlinger
Redaktion: Gesa Füßle
Fachredaktion: Alison Frankland
Produktion: Wolfram Friedrich
Titelillustration: Karl Knospe
Typographischer Entwurf: Maria Seidel
Umschlaggestaltung: Carsten Abelbeck

ISBN 978-3-8174-7763-0
7277633

Besuchen Sie uns im Internet: www.compactverlag.de, www.lernkrimi.de

Vorwort

Mit dem neuen, spannenden Compact Lernkrimi können Sie Ihre Englischkenntnisse auf schnelle und einfache Weise vertiefen, auffrischen und überprüfen.
Inspector Hudson erleichtert das Sprachtraining mit Action und Humor.
Der Lernkrimi „Schüsse im Nebel“ ist die Siegerstory des zweiten großen Compact-Krimi-Schreibwettbewerbs.
Der Krimi wird auf jeder Seite durch abwechslungsreiche und kurzweilige Übungen ergänzt, die das Lernen unterhaltsam und spannend machen. Prüfen Sie Ihr Englisch in Lückentexten, Zuordnungs- und Übersetzungsaufgaben, in Buchstabenspielen und Kreuzworträtseln!
Ob im Bus oder in der Bahn, im Wartezimmer, zu Hause oder in der Mittagspause – das Sprachtraining im handlichen Format bietet die ideale Trainingsmöglichkeit für zwischendurch.
Schreiben Sie die Lösungen einfach ins Buch!
Die richtigen Antworten sind in einem eigenen Lösungsteil am Ende des Buches zusammengefasst. Im Anhang befindet sich außerdem ein Glossar, in dem die schwierigsten Wörter übersetzt sind. Diese sind im Text kursiv markiert.

Und nun kann die Spannung beginnen …

Viel Spaß und Erfolg!

Die Ereignisse und die handelnden Personen in diesem Buch sind frei erfunden. Etwaige Ähnlichkeiten mit tatsächlichen Ereignissen oder lebenden Personen wären rein zufällig und unbeabsichtigt.

Inhalt

Story

James Hudson arbeitet als Inspector bei der legendären Polizeibehörde Scotland Yard. Er ist einer der fähigsten Männer und wird immer dann zurate gezogen, wenn seine Kollegen mal wieder vor einem Rätsel stehen. Dieses Mal geht es darum, ein Verbrechen im geheimnisvollen Moor aufzuklären, bei dem ihm auch Elvira Elliot, die junge, attraktive Versicherungsagentin, zur Seite steht.

Jessica Langer, das Au-pair-Mädchen bei den Lockwoods, hört beim Joggen plötzlich zwei Schüsse. Kurz darauf ist Mr. Smith, der Freund und Chef von Mr. Lockwood, spurlos verschwunden. Haben die Schüsse etwas mit dem Verschwinden von Mr. Smith zu tun? Und wer steckt dahinter? Etwa Mr. Smiths Sekretärin und heimliche Geliebte, deren eifersüchtiger Freund oder gar ein anderer Mitarbeiter? Inspector Hudson und Sergeant Wood tappen zunächst im Dunkeln, bis Jessica ihnen einen hilfreichen Hinweis liefert …

Chapter 1: Strange Conversation

Jessica Langer was helping Mrs Lockwood in the kitchen. They were getting the main course ready for dinner. In the background she could hear the guests talking and laughing. Mrs Lockwood took the steak pie out of the oven and placed the *steaming* dish on the kitchen worktop.

"Looks nice, eh?" she said with a smile.

Jessica smiled back and *nodded*. She was being a little *dishonest* because she did not actually care too much for British food. In fact, after a year as an au pair at the Lockwoods', she was quite fed up with it. She was looking forward to her mother's excellent cooking when she got back to Germany. Not long to go, just one more week and then it would be goodbye, England. Jessica was enjoying her stay at the Lockwoods', they were very nice people; however, she felt homesick and was looking forward to returning to Germany.

"Could you please take the *brussel sprouts* out of the pan and put them on the plates?" Mrs Lockwood asked her.

"Yes, of course," she answered.

Jessica walked over to the oven, which stood right beside the window. She began putting the *brussel sprouts* on the plates. Jessica looked out of the window.

"It's really foggy out there," she said.

"Yes, I know," answered Mrs Lockwood. "It's enough to *give you the creeps*. Just as well we're in our *cosy* little house."

Thick, grey-white *mist* was *spreading out*, reaching for the house like a thousand helpless *pale* hands wanting to *drag* the *abode* into the dark *uncanny* moors. Jessica could never really get used to the *mist*. The *mist* was created by the moors nearby. It often blurred the view of the comforting *scenery* of fields and trees. *Laughter roared* again from the dining room. John Lockwood's deep jovial laugh could be heard above all.

"They're having a good time, aren't they?" Mrs Lockwood smiled.

"They sure are," replied Jessica.

"I'm so glad John has found his humour again," Mrs Lockwood *carried on*. "The last couple of weeks he has seemed so *distracted* and nervous. I guess he's just had a lot of work," she sighed.

Jessica agreed. Mr Lockwood had seemed very *preoccupied* for the last couple of weeks, not at all his usual talkative and humorous self.

! ÜBUNG 1

Übung 1: Welche Gegenteile gehören zusammen? Ordnen Sie zu!

1. ☐ dishonest	a) walk
2. ☐ enjoy	b) pale
3. ☐ foggy	c) blurred
4. ☐ rough	d) honest
5. ☐ run	e) preoccupied
6. ☐ give	f) sorry
7. ☐ colourful	g) smooth
8. ☐ clear	h) sunny
9. ☐ glad	i) take
10. ☐ carefree	j) hate

They took the main course out and served it.

"Mmm, that looks lovely!" Mr Smith said.

"Yes, just delicious!" Mrs Smith remarked.

Mr and Mrs Lockwood smiled at each other warmly. Jessica sat down. She was dining with them. Mr and Mrs Lockwood were always very kind and treated her almost like a member of the family. Mr Smith picked up his glass.

"I would like to *propose a toast*," he said. "Thank you for being such great hosts. It's always a pleasure to be here."
"It's always a pleasure to have you," Mr Lockwood replied.
"I'm so glad you didn't mind me getting the job you were after. I always thought, that man is going to hate me," Mr Smith joked. "But now we are friends."
Mr Lockwood smiled. He felt a little uncomfortable, but tried to hide this feeling as well as he could.
"Some you win, some you lose" he replied jovially.
The crystal glasses clinked, creating an *erratic* tune. Then everybody picked up their *cutlery* and started to eat.
Mr Smith was Mr Lockwood's boss at the local bank. He actually got the job Mr Lockwood thought he was getting, but, to his *disappointment*, he missed out. Mr Lockwood did not let Mr Smith feel this, but in a way, he *resented* the man; additionally, Mr Smith was five years younger than him. However, he knew it was important to get on well with him. In fact, as time went by, they actually became something like friends, *occasionally* having each other round for dinner and playing squash every Monday against each other – Mr Smith usually won.
Suddenly Kevin, their five year old son, appeared at the table. He was holding his teddy in one hand and rubbing his eyes with the other.
"Mummy, I can't sleep," he said.
As Mrs Lockwood was about to get up, Jessica stopped her.
"It's all right; I'll take care of him", she insisted. "I can take him back to bed."
Jessica took Kevin by the hand and led him upstairs.
"She's such a pet," Mrs Lockwood said to her husband.
"Yes!" he answered with his mouth full. "Don't know what we're going to do without her."

When they got upstairs, Kevin all of a sudden started to *head for* the bedroom of his sister Barbara, who was three years older than him.

"What are you doing?" whispered Jessica.

"Maybe Barbara wants to hear a good night story as well," he answered excitedly.

Jessica ran along the hall and managed to stop him just in time before he opened her door.

"I think she's asleep and so should you be," she smiled.

Kevin *shrugged*, took Jessica's hand and walked *obediently* with her towards his room.

ÜBUNG 2 !

Übung 2: Welches Wort ist das „schwarze Schaf"? Unterstreichen Sie das nicht in die Reihe passende Wort!

1. son, father, mother, brother
2. I, you, his, me
3. erratic, incoherent, consistent, irregular
4. dark, night, bright, gloomy
5. say, answer, speak, talk
6. dreaming, awake, asleep, snore
7. obey, follow, do, decline
8. mouth, teeth, lips, tongue

Jessica picked up the *nursery rhyme book* she had been reading to him on previous occasions.

"No, no, I know all of them. I want you tell me a new story, one I've never heard before," Kevin said.

"But Kevin, it's late and…" Jessica answered.

"Oh please!" he *begged* her.

"All right then," Jessica *gave in.*
She looked out of Kevin's bedroom window. The *mist* was as thick as ever. An animal made an *eerie* noise in the distance. Jessica turned back to Kevin and *tucked him in*. He smiled. He was really looking forward to hearing the story. Jessica liked making up stories.
"*Once upon a time*," she began, "there was a little Prince who lived in a castle near the moors…"
"Is that me, am I the Prince!" Kevin *interrupted.*
"Perhaps!" Jessica joked. "But let me tell the story."
Kevin put his head back on his pillow.
"It was always *misty* out on the moors," she continued. "In fact, the thick *mist* never went away. Because of this, the Prince had to stay close to the castle. He was never allowed to walk into the *mist*. However, the Prince could never stop thinking about what may be beyond the *mist*. There were legends that dangerous *dragons* lived out there and that they *particularly* liked to eat little boys…"
"Oh, oh!" Kevin remarked, slipping underneath his covers.
Jessica laughed.

Übung 3: Bilden Sie die korrekte ing-Form!

1. prefer preferring
2. take taking
3. hum humming
4. run running
5. lie ~~lieng~~ lying
6. travel travelling

ÜBUNG 3 !

7. die dying

8. get getting

9. sit sitting

"One day, the little Prince was playing with his ball. He *accidentally* kicked his ball over the castle walls. There was nobody around who he could ask to get it, so he ran to the castle gate. It was locked. 'How am I supposed to get my ball back?' the Prince wondered. He looked up at the gate. It was very high. He *gathered* all his *courage* and started to climb up the gate…"

"I'd do that too, I really would," *boasted* Kevin.

Jessica smiled.

"I have *no doubts* about that," she replied. "He climbed over the gate to the other side. He searched along the wall for his ball, but he could not find it. Then suddenly he thought he could *make it out.* It was almost hidden by the *mist*. The Prince started to run in the direction of the ball. Then he hesitated. His mother had told him not to go into the *mist* – it was dangerous. However, the Prince wanted his favourite ball back more than anything else in the world and he walked into the thick cloud of *mist*. Strangely, his ball was gone. He turned around in circles, but it was nowhere to be seen. The Prince walked further into the fog. But he could not find his ball. This made him very sad. Eventually he decided to go back home. The Prince walked and walked, but the clouds of *dense mist* just would not get thinner. His home was nowhere in sight. He started to run, but he could see nothing but white, *dense* fog, no matter where he looked. The Prince was beginning to get afraid. And suddenly he heard a big, loud bang…"

Kevin slipped under his covers even further.

"Will he be safe?" he asked, worriedly.
"If I tell you now, there's not really much point in telling you the story," Jessica said.
"Okay, I was just asking," answered Kevin, a little *disappointed*.
"The Prince got a great fright," Jessica *carried on*. "What was that noise?" he asked himself. It sounded like a *giant dragon spitting fire*. He could also hear its feet *pounding* on the ground. The ground was shaking. The Prince started to run. He did not know where he was going, but as long as it was far enough away from the *dragon*, he would be happy. However, no matter how fast he ran, the beast seemed to be coming closer. By now the Prince was very frightened. He swore that if he got back alive, he would never go back into the moors. As he ran, he turned around to see if he could see the *dragon*. But it was nowhere to be seen. He could hear it, though. The Prince ran as fast as he could, then suddenly, the moment he thought all was lost, he saw the castle in the distance. Suddenly the *pounding* stopped. He turned around. The *dragon* seemed to have given up. The Prince ran towards the gates. To his *bewilderment,* his ball came flying out of the *mist*, hit the gates with a thundering noise, *bounced off* them and came to a halt. The Prince looked out into the *mist* in amazement. 'Can *dragons* play football?' he wondered. It certainly was a good shot. 'We don't play football out here!' a loud, deep and heavy voice suddenly said. 'Sorry, I did not know that,' the little Prince answered. He *grabbed* his ball, turned back around and *scrambled* up the gates. When he got to the other side, he felt safe. 'You don't like to play, do you?' the Prince asked in a *cheeky* voice. There was no answer. 'Oh, well then,' the Prince continued. 'I don't care anyway, you stupid *dragon*!'"
Kevin *chuckled*. He liked the *cheekiness* of the little Prince. Jessica smiled back.

ÜBUNG 4 !

Übung 4: Übersetzen Sie! Achten Sie dabei auf die richtige Präposition!

1. in der Schule — at school
2. mit dem Flugzeug — by plane
3. aus London — from london
4. am Sonntag — on Sunday
5. am Himmel — ~~at the sky~~ in the sky
6. am Morgen — ~~at~~ in the morning
7. in der Nacht — ~~in~~ at the night
8. auf dem Tisch — ~~at~~ on the table
9. im 21. Jahrhundert — in the 21. ~~century~~ century
10. im Alter von — ~~with~~ at the age of

"Then suddenly, the *dragon* appeared out of the *mist*. It was about six metres tall and its skin had a *greenish*, red colour…"

"*Yuck!*" Kevin exclaimed.

"…The Prince was *trembling*. 'Sorry, I didn't mean to be…' *Horrified*, he watched the *dragon* fly over the gate towards him. 'Oh no, he's going to eat me!' the Prince thought. However, the *dragon* just lifted up his ball with its *claws*, flew back into the air and hit the ball with his wing. The Prince watched in amazement as the ball shot through the sky like a rocket. 'Wow!' he exclaimed. 'We play wing-ball,' the *dragon* said, *roaring with laughter*…"

"Wing-ball?" said Kevin, slightly puzzled. "Never heard of it."

"Well, now you have," answered Jessica with a *grin*.
"So what happened, did the *dragon* eat the boy?"
"No," replied Jessica. "He *disappeared* back into the *mist*."
"And the Prince?"
"The Prince was never *cheeky* again," answered Jessica.
"Never again?"
"Yes," Jessica *nodded knowingly*.
"That's tough," Kevin remarked.
He *yawned*.
"I think it's time for you to go to sleep now."
"But…"
"No buts!" Jessica said. "It's very late."
"All right!"
Kevin lay down. Jessica kissed him on the *forehead* and walked towards the door. She opened it. One could hear talking and laughing from downstairs. Jessica switched the bedroom light off.
"Jessica?" Kevin asked, just before she closed the door.
"Yes?"
"Is there really a dangerous *dragon* out there on the moors?"
"No, of course not. It's just a story," Jessica replied.
"Good!" Kevin said.
"Good night, Kevin," Jessica said and closed the door.
Jessica *yawned*. She was tired, too. I'll just *skip* dessert and go to bed, she thought. Jessica went downstairs and walked into the dining room.
"You missed dessert, girl!" Mr Smith said jovially.
He appeared to be a little drunk.
"That's okay, I think I'll be going to bed now anyway," Jessica replied.
"Really, dear," Mrs Lockwood said. "We were just going to have some cheese and biscuits.

"No, I'm fine thank you, good night!" Jessica said.
"Good night!" everybody said.

Jessica closed the door behind her and walked back upstairs. She went into the bathroom and washed her face. Then she brushed her teeth. As she entered her room, she *wrinkled her nose*. What was that awful smell? It was cigarette smoke. She realized her window was still open. She shivered. The tobacco smell was coming form outside.
"Damn, I forgot to close it!" Jessica exclaimed.
She hurried to close her window. Jessica saw dark shadows appearing below. They belonged to Mr Lockwood and Mr Smith. The two men were standing in the garden smoking cigarettes. Jessica *tutted*. She hated cigarettes. Just as she was about to close her window, she could not help overhearing part of the conversation.
"I don't know what you are talking about!" said Mr Lockwood irritably.
"I think you do, John!" answered Mr Smith.
Mr Lockwood whispered something to Mr Smith which Jessica could not hear. She leaned further out of the window, trying hard to find out what the two men were talking about. Suddenly she slipped. She *bumped* her head on the half-open window. Jessica quickly ducked. At the same moment, the two men looked up. They did not see her *disappear*. Jessica hid beneath the window. Mr Smith pointed at a pigeon on the roof. Mr Lockwood looked *relieved*. For a moment he thought someone was *spying on* them.
"Now, what I was saying…" Mr Lockwood continued, somewhat more calmly.
Jessica carefully *peeked* over the *windowsill*. Again she tried to listen, but unfortunately they walked away from her window, further into the garden, *disappearing* into the fog.

Übung 5: Wie heißt das Simple Past der folgenden unregelmäßigen Verben?

1. be was
2. get got
3. go went
4. hear ~~heart~~ heard
5. fall ~~felt~~ fell
6. come came
7. do did
8. eat ate
9. let let
10. say said

Chapter 2: Shots in the Mist

The next day was like any other day: Mr Lockwood left the house early. The children were running through the house. They were laughing and joking. Kevin still just had one sock on and Jessica was running after him, trying to *make him put the other sock on*.
"Kevin, come over here, right now!" Jessica exclaimed.
But all Kevin did was *make funny faces* and run away.
"So you haven't learnt anything at all," Jessica said.
"Learnt what?" Kevin asked.
"What happens to *cheeky* boys," she answered. "Do you remember the Prince?"

"Nothing really happened to him, did it?"
"I didn't finish the whole story, did I?"
"So what happens?"
Jessica started running in Kevin's direction, making *pretend dragon* noises. Kevin *screeched* and ran away. Jessica got him and lifted him off the ground. She bit playfully into his *stomach*. This made Kevin *giggle*.
"He ate him all up!" Jessica exclaimed.
"Okay, okay, I'll get my socks on," Kevin laughed.
Jessica put him back down on the ground and put his other sock on. While this was all happening, Mrs Lockwood was sitting quietly in the *study* writing her latest novel. She wasn't actually a famous writer, although she had won some prizes by participating in short story competitions. However, to her regret, she had not yet published a novel. But she wasn't one to give up that easily and writing was something she enjoyed very much.

ÜBUNG 6 !

Übung 6: Benutzen Sie die Kurzform!

1. I cannot	I can't
2. That is	That's
3. I do not	I don't
4. you are	you're
5. we will	we'll
6. it is	it's
7. could not	couldn't
8. I am	I'm

9. he is he's

10. does not doesn't

Later that afternoon, Jessica felt like going jogging. She really needed some fresh air. Jessica knocked on the *study* door.
"Come in!" Mrs Lockwood said.
Jessica entered the *study*.
"Would you mind if I went jogging before dinner, Mrs Lockwood?"
"No, no, I don't mind," she answered cheerfully.
"How's the writing coming along?"
"Great, thank you! Another 50 pages to go and then I'm finished!" she *beamed*.
"Sounds good, I'll be off then."
"Okay, have fun!"
Just as Jessica was about to close the door, Mrs Lockwood called:
"Oh, and be back in half an hour. Dinner will be ready by then," Mrs Lockwood called after her.
"Okay, will do," Jessica replied.
Great! she thought, while closing the *study* door. That's not really much time. I'll have to *get a move on*.
Jessica hurried upstairs and put on her jogging outfit quickly.

Übung 7: Schreiben Sie die Uhrzeit aus!

ÜBUNG 7 !

1. 07:30 half past seven

2. 11:10 ten past eleven

3. 03:15 quarter past three

4. 12:00 a.m. twelve o'clock

5. 13:45 quarter to two

6. 02:55 five to three

7. 05:06 six past five

As she closed the front door behind her, she noticed that it was extremely *misty*. She wondered whether she should just go back inside. The density of the *mist* made her feel uncomfortable. However, going for a run was better than watching the children's favourite film for the tenth time. She switched on her MP3 player and started to run. As the *mist* was so thick, she was careful not to *lose her way*. Jessica kept to the *paths meandering* through the moor. It was a little *uncanny*. She could not see very far, trees and bushes appeared out of nowhere – the branches sometimes pulling at her *hooded jumper*, as if deliberately trying to slow her down. She tried to *distract* herself with pleasant thoughts. Jessica started thinking about home, her family, her boyfriend. She missed him very much and could hardly wait to see him again. Suddenly Jessica heard something that sounded like a shot. She came to a sudden halt and removed the earphones from her ears.
"What on earth was that?" she exclaimed.
It was silent again. Jessica listened. She could hear nothing but the music coming from the headphones connected to her MP3 player. She *shrugged*. Maybe she *was mistaken*. Then suddenly another shot resounded. Jessica *cringed*. She scanned the surrounding area, but the *mist* made it impossible for her to see anything. Her blood was *pounding* in her ears. Jessica panicked and started to run for her life in the direction she thought the house to be in. On the way she stumbled over tree roots. She got back on her feet and *sped*

around a corner. Jessica saw the turn too late, left the trail, slipped on the wet grass and fell headfirst into a *jagged* bush.

"Ouch!" she cried.

Her face was scratched, but there was no time to pay any attention to her wounds. Jessica *scrambled* to her feet again and rushed back to the *path*. Only when she reached it did she start to feel the stabbing pain in her chest. Her face was *throbbing*. She was panting for breath. Jessica sank onto the front door step. She felt *dizzy* and was shaking all over. A few minutes later, after regaining some of her self control, she stood up and opened the door. Mrs Lockwood was standing in the hallway. She looked at her, worried.

"What happened to you?" she asked.

"I heard shots…I thought someone was shooting at me…!" Jessica exclaimed, with a little more fear in her voice than she really intended to show.

Jessica was still shaking slightly. Mrs Lockwood helped the poor girl in. Just as she was entering, Mr Lockwood turned up at the door. He had just come home from work and was dressed in his shirt and tie. Mr Lockwood looked a little *paler* that usual. He put his briefcase down.

"Good gracious, what has happened to you, girl?!" he exclaimed.

"John, she said she thinks someone was shooting at her!"

"Where?"

"Out on the moor while she was jogging."

Mr Lockwood looked at Jessica and then at his wife. Then all of a sudden, his pensiveness broke into a smile. He laughed. The girl and woman looked at him, astounded, wondering what on earth could be so funny about nearly being shot.

"It's the *hunting season* just now, it was probably a hunter shooting some *deer*," he explained.

Mrs Lockwood looked *relieved*.

"That's right, dear," she said reassuringly to Jessica, who still looked frightened.
Jessica smiled.
"How silly of me…But is it not a little dangerous, shooting out there when it is so *misty*? One can hardly see one's hand in front of one's face."
"She is right!" agreed Mrs Lockwood. "Imagine if Barbara and Kevin had been playing outside. I'll lodge a complaint first thing tomorrow!"
"Oh, that's okay, darling. I'll take care of that."
And with that, Mr Lockwood picked up his briefcase, walked into the house and closed the door behind him. Jessica could not help noticing that his briefcase was much more *bulky* than usual.
He must have a lot of work to do again, she thought, *recalling* the *amount* of paperwork he had been through during the last couple of weeks.

! ÜBUNG 8

Übung 8: Übersetzen Sie die Wörter in Klammern!

Jessica *retired* to bed (1. früh) ______ that night, her face burning slightly from the scratches. Jessica's arm was also *sore*. (2. glücklicherweise) ______ she hadn't broken it, she thought to herself. Jessica closed her eyes.
"What a day". "That crazy (3. Jäger) ______ *scared the living daylights out of* me."
The phone rang downstairs. Jessica shot up. It was probably her boyfriend Mark. He said he would call and (4. niemand) ______

else ever really called the Lockwoods at this time in the (5. Abend) evening ______. She hurried to the door. How she longed to (6. teilen) share ______ her scary experience with him. Jessica rushed downstairs, but by the time she got there, Mrs Lockwood had already picked up the (7. Hörer) ______.

"Hello, Janet!" she said.

Jessica felt (8. enttäuscht) sad x ______.

I hope they don't (9. plaudern) talk x chatter ______ all night, she thought.

Just as she was about to turn around and go back upstairs, something Mrs Lockwood said caught her attention:
"No, Martin's not here… I see… That is strange… Yes… But I'm certain he'll turn up… Yes, will do… Yes, goodbye."
Mrs Lockwood replaced the *receiver*. Mr Lockwood *peeked* out of the *study*.
"Everything all right, dear?" he asked.
"I'm not quite sure," she answered thoughtfully. "That was Janet Smith. Martin should have been home three hours ago. She has no idea where he could be. His mobile seems to be turned off and he's not at the office. Do you know anything?"
"Don't *have a clue*. I left the office earlier today because I had an *appointment* with a customer."
"I hope nothing has happened!" she said worriedly.
Jessica turned around and slowly walked back upstairs.
What a *weird* day, she was thinking as she opened her bedroom door. She fell asleep.

ÜBUNG 9 !

Übung 9: Unterstreichen und verbessern Sie im folgenden Textabschnitt die sechs falsch geschriebenen Wörter!

Then the phone rang again. Her heart leeped. Was it Mark this time? To her great joy it was.

"I'll take the call upstairs," Jessica said.

Mrs Lockwood dialled number two and the phone started to ring in the hall upstairs. Jessica piked up the *receiver*.

"Hi there, Jess! How's it going, how's your English coming along?" her boyfriend asked.

He was from Amerika, so they usually spoke English together.

"Something dreadful happened today," Jessica said.

"What?"

"I heard shots when I was out on the moors," she ansered.

"Shots?" he asked in a surprised voice. "Are you okay?"

"Yes, I'm fine now. But it *frightened the hell out of me*."

"Is it *hunting season* over there?"

"I've no idea. That's what Mr Lockwood said, anyway."

"It's time you came home, I mis you."

"Yes, I know. It's not long. I can't wait myself."

"Are you sure you're okay?" her boyfriend asked caringly.

"Yes, I'm fine. Let's change the subject. How was the movie the other night?"

1. ____________ 4. ____________

2. ____________ 5. ____________

3. ____________ 6. ____________

"It was great. You should definitely watch it."

Jessica just let him talk on. She smiled warmly.

Chapter 3: Close to Murder

It was very early in the morning. Inspector Hudson was trying to find his way through a thick, white blanket of fog. He stopped and rubbed his hands together. It was very cold.

I *haven't the foggiest idea* where my colleagues are, he thought. How am I supposed to find them in this?

Then he smiled and thought about what had just gone through his head: 'Foggiest', you couldn't say it better.

Inspector Hudson walked on. Then, to his *relief*, he could see the outlines of his colleagues. The *mist* made it impossible for him to tell who was who. All of a sudden, a flashlight went off and for a second he could see the body lying on the ground. Inspector Hudson walked over to them. Sergeant Wood saw his superior *approaching* and went to greet him. "Good morning, Sir." he said.

"Good morning, Sergeant. What have we got?" Inspector Hudson inquired.

"The victim's name is Martin Smith."

Inspector Hudson looked at the body. Martin Smith's face was *pale* and had a frozen look of shock on it, as if whatever had happened to him had taken him totally by surprise. His coat was open – the dead man's white shirt was covered in blood and dirt. Inspector Hudson had seen many dead bodies in his time, but he still could never get used to the sight – this soulless clump of matter *spread out* before him.

ÜBUNG 10 !

Übung 10: Fügen Sie die richtigen Präpositionen ein!
(in, into, near, over, at, under, on)

1. Jessica was in______ the house.

2. He walked ______ to them.

3. The body was lying ______ the ground.

4. The policemen were ______ the body.

5. His chest was ______ his shirt.

6. Inspector Hudson was ______ the crime scene.

7. He disappeared ______ the mist.

"He was shot twice: once in the *stomach* and once in the chest. The *bullet* in his chest killed him."

"Did you find the weapon?"

"Negative, Sir, no weapon. The *bullets* are pretty big, so it must have been a *rifle* or something similar."

"How long has he been dead?"

"It's difficult to say, maybe around twelve hours. He was reported missing by his wife yesterday evening at 8:00 p.m. Of course, as you know, no *search warrant* was issued, as we never do until after 24 hours."

All of a sudden there was a *commotion*. A group of people were coming towards the crime scene. Inspector Hudson *recognised* one of them.

"How did they find out so quickly?"

Sergeant Wood turned around.

"Not that slimy journalist, Howard Geek?"

A *stout* man, his *greasy* hair combed back, came hurrying towards him.

"Now tell me, Inspector, how…"

"No comment!" Inspector Hudson growled. "Sergeant Wood, please have your men remove these gentlemen straight away."

Sergeant Wood called over some *constables*. They forced the men back.

"But you can't just…" protested Howard Geek.

"Oh yes I can!" smiled Inspector Hudson. "This is a crime scene, you can't just burst in. Show some respect."

Inspector Hudson didn't like journalists very much. They sometimes behaved like animals – almost willing to kill for a great story and showing no respect for the victims whatsoever. The *constables* closed off the crime scene. Some of the reporters were holding up their cameras over the policemen's heads, trying to get a photograph.

"Do you know where Martin Smith lived?"

"Yes, Cobble Field Road."

"Well, let's get there quickly, before his poor wife finds out about her husband's death on the 12:00 o'clock news."

Mrs Smith was sitting on the couch. Across from her sat Inspector Hudson and Sergeant Wood. She appeared to be pretty calm for someone who had just heard that her husband was dead.

"I have no idea why he was killed," Mrs Smith said.

"Did you notice any changes in his behaviour *recently*?" the inspector asked.

"No, he was his usual self. He was the happy type, you know. Always in a *good mood*, telling jokes, making other people laugh…"

Mrs Smith started to cry. Inspector Hudson gave her a handkerchief. She blew her nose.

"On Friday, the day of his…"

Mrs Smith *dabbed* the tears from her eyes.

"I'm sorry," she said.

"Take your time," Inspector Hudson said sympathetically.

Mrs Smith *took a deep breath.*

! ÜBUNG 11

Übung 11: Setzen Sie die richtigen Fragepronomen ein!
(who (2x), whose, which, where (2x), what)

1. Who ________ is Mr Lockwood?
2. In which ________ part of the moor was Mr Smith killed?
3. what ________ happened to Jessica?
4. where ________ did Mr Smith work?
5. who ________ is Mr Lockwood's boss?
6. whose ________ rifle is that?
7. whre ________ did the bullets come from?

"On Friday, he left the house at the usual time. That's always around 8:30 a.m. I remember he called me around lunchtime. He told me he would be home at dinner time. That was the last I heard from him."

Mrs Smith started to cry again. Inspector Hudson and Sergeant Wood waited a moment before *carrying on with* the questioning.

"I know this is not easy," Inspector Hudson said. "If you want us to come again later, it's no problem."

Mrs Smith shook her head.

"No, no. It's okay, *carry on*."

"When exactly is dinner time?"

"Well, he usually came home at 6:00 p.m. Dinner was served a little later."

"After you realised he was late, did you call him at the bank?"

"Yes, but there was nobody left at the bank. It was nearly 6:30 p.m. He did tell me that he had an *appointment* that day, though."

"When?" asked Inspector Hudson.

"I think just after four, if I remember correctly. I called him on his mobile. I could hear he was in the car. He told me he was on his way to an *appointment*."

Sergeant Hudson wrote this down in his book.

"Do you know where or with whom?"

"No, I'm sorry. Maybe his secretary knows more."

"What is his secretary's name?"

"Miss Olivia Anderson."

Her voice had a slight note of *resentment* in it. Inspector Hudson raised his eyebrow. Sergeant Wood *jotted down* the name.

"Thank you very much!" said the inspector as he *got to his feet.* "We don't want to *strain* you too much."

The sergeant got up as well.

Mrs Smith accompanied the policemen to the door.

"Please keep me updated on the latest news," she said, trying to sound *composed*.

They all shook hands. Mrs Smith closed the door. As soon as it snapped into the *lock*, she started to *sob*.

Übung 12: Wie heißt das Wort auf Englisch?

ÜBUNG 12 !

1. Atem ______________________
2. Verhalten ______________________
3. Witze ______________________
4. fortfahren ______________________
5. Termin ______________________
6. anstrengen ______________________

Sergeant Wood parked the police car outside the bank.
"Did you notice that tone in her voice, Sir, when Mrs Smith gave us the name of the secretary?" Sergeant Wood asked.
"Yes, I did. It sounded kind of *resentful* to me, but I didn't want to say anything. The poor woman needed a break," replied the inspector.
Sergeant Wood *nodded*. The policemen got out of the car.
"We'll look into that later," Inspector Hudson said. "Maybe it didn't mean a thing. But on the other hand, it usually does. Doesn't it, Sergeant?"
"It sure does," he answered.
They closed the doors and walked towards the bank.

ÜBUNG 13

Übung 13: Welche Wörter gehören zusammen? Ordnen Sie zu!

1. ☐ dinner	a) head
2. ☐ body	b) outside
3. ☐ nod	c) dark
4. ☐ trees	d) tears
5. ☐ late	e) plates
6. ☐ handkerchief	f) death
7. ☐ car	g) shot
8. ☐ gun	h) street

As Inspector Hudson and Sergeant Wood entered the bank, they could feel that the atmosphere was tense and full of *dismay*. Many people seemed to be shocked. Some of the employees even had red eyes. They looked at the policemen. People whispered as they walked by.
"Looks like they know something already," commented Sergeant Wood. "Let us have a look."

"Yes, and I have a slight *suspicion* as to who could be the *source*."
Inspector Hudson *nodded* in the direction of a counter. There stood Howard Geek, talking to a bank employee and *jotting down* notes.
"Get him out of here!" exclaimed Inspector Hudson.
"My pleasure, Sir," replied the sergeant.
Sergeant Wood *approached* Howard Geek and *interrupted* him in the middle of a sentence.
"I must ask you to leave, Mr Geek," the sergeant said.
"I'm in the middle of an interview!" Howard Geek complained.
"Now!" Sergeant Wood replied *firmly*.
Howard Geek put his writing pad into his inner jacket pocket.
"You are undermining the freedom of speech!"
"You can say what you want, Mr Geek. However, please do so outside!"
Sergeant Wood pointed in the direction of the exit.
"This is the second time today that you've been hindering police investigations. Next time we might not be so *polite*."
"*Polite*?" *spat* Howard Geek. "You must be joking!"
The journalist headed towards the door. He turned back, giving the policemen a dirty look, then left the bank. Sergeant Wood turned to the man Howard Geek had just been interviewing.
"Could you please tell me where to find Miss Anderson?"
"Is it really true then?" the man asked sadly.
"I'm afraid so," replied the sergeant.
"Good God!" the employee exclaimed.
He paused and *gathered himself together*.
"Second floor, last office on the right. That is also…"
The bank clerk cleared his throat.
"I mean that was also where Mr Smith's office was."
Inspector Hudson and Sergeant Wood headed for the lift.
The moment Inspector Hudson and Sergeant Wood saw Miss

Olivia Anderson, they understood why Mrs Smith might feel a little *resentful* towards her. Olivia Anderson was a very pretty woman. She wore a short dress, showing off her long, slim legs. Her curly, dark hair was tied in a bow. Sergeant Wood could not help admiring her beautifully curved, aristocratic neck. Miss Anderson was standing beside her desk, sorting out some papers. She looked up. Her dark, cat-like eyes were red.

"Miss Anderson?" inquired Inspector Hudson.

"Yes," she replied.

"I am Inspector Hudson and this is Sergeant Wood."

The Sergeant smiled politely.

"We are *investigating* the murder of Mr Smith."

The woman *nodded* slightly. She seemed somewhat *distracted*. Her moves were trancelike and delayed.

"Oh yes, I see… Please sit down."

The inspector and Sergeant Wood took a seat. Miss Anderson sat down, too.

"When did you last see Mr Smith?" asked Inspector Hudson.

"It must have been around 4:00 p.m. That was not his style. He was a hard worker and always the last to leave the office – even on Fridays."

"So he didn't have an *appointment*, then?" asked Sergeant Wood reading through his notes.

"No, not that I know of," replied Miss Anderson.

Sergeant Wood and Inspector Hudson exchanged looks.

"So Mr Smith had no *appointments* on this day?" Inspector Hudson asked.

"No."

"What did he say before he left?"

"He said he needed to *run* a few *errands*. And that he'd be back."

"But he never returned?"

"No."

Olivia Anderson started to cry. She took a tissue and wiped her eyes.

"Did this not appear strange to you?"

"A little, but who am I to tell my boss when to come and go?"

"Did you notice anything strange in his behaviour?"

"Not really… But wait… Just before he left he *received* a call on his mobile. I didn't hear what he was talking about, but he did seem a little irritated about something."

Übung 14: Geben Sie die verneinte Form in ihrer Kurzform an!

ÜBUNG 14 !

1. They are	They aren't
2. He is	He isn't
3. We did	We didn't
4. She will	She ~~would~~ won't
5. It can	It can't
6. They would	They wouldn't
7. I have killed	I ~~don't~~ haven't killed

At this moment Mr Lockwood entered the office.

"Good morning, Miss Anderson!" he said happily.

He looked startled the moment he saw the state of Miss Anderson and the policemen.

"Is everything okay?"

Miss Anderson shook her head.

"Have you not heard yet?"

"Heard what? I've just come up in the lift from the underground car park."

"Martin Smith has been murdered," said Inspector Hudson.

Mr Lockwood looked *stunned*.

"This is some kind of joke, right?" he said.

"I wish it was," replied the inspector.

"But… I mean… Who would do such a thing?"

"That's what we're here to find out," said Inspector Hudson very seriously.

"Where did it happen?" Mr Lockwood asked.

"Out on the moors."

"On the moors? But what on earth was he doing out there?"

Mr Lockwood paused.

"Wait a minute… My au pair, Jessica, said she heard something out on the moors while she was jogging."

"What did she hear?" inquired the inspector.

"She *claimed* that she heard shots, she was very *intimidated* by the whole experience…I thought it was a hunter."

"Shots?" Inspector Hudson asked. "How many?"

"Two, I think, maybe three, I can't remember."

The inspector and the sergeant exchanged looks again.

"When was this?"

"As I said, yesterday, around five o'clock in the evening."

"Will she be at home just now?" he inquired.

"I think so," replied Mr Lockwood.

Inspector Hudson and the sergeant got up.

"Thank you very much for your cooperation," Inspector Hudson said. "I'm sure we'll have some more questions in the near future."

"Yes, if there's anything we can do…" answered Mr Lockwood. He suddenly seemed *lost for words.*

The policemen said goodbye and left the bank.

Übung 15: Ergänzen Sie die fehlenden Verbformen!

Infinitive	Simple Past	Past Participle
1. meet	met	met
2. run	ran	run
3. Say	said	said
4. make	made	made
5. keep	kept	kept
6. knew	know	known
7. think	thought	thought

"It's strange that Mr Smith told his wife he was on his way to an *appointment* and his secretary knows nothing about it," remarked Sergeant Wood.

"Yes, it is. There was obviously something *odd* going on; his phone rang just before he left suddenly. He seemed somewhat irritated. Nobody knows where he went. A few hours later he was shot out on the moors."

"If we're lucky we might have a *witness*," Sergeant Wood said.

"Yes, maybe," replied Inspector Hudson.

The policemen got into the car.

Chapter 4: Out on the Moor

For a change, it was clearer now out on the moors. Inspector Hudson walked along with Jessica by his side. Green, *marshy* land stretched before them as far as the eye could see. To their left was a small lake. It was surrounded by slim, naked trees. Jessica had still not quite taken in what had happened to Mr Smith.

"Tell me, Jessica," Inspector Hudson asked in a careful, friendly tone. "Where exactly where you when you heard the shots?"

"It was near here. I remember because the small lake was nearby. However, I couldn't tell you precisely where I was."

Jessica jumped. She didn't realise that there were divers in the lake. Inspector Hudson saw her surprised look.

"Police divers," he explained. "They're searching the water for the weapon."

ÜBUNG 16

Übung 16: Welches Wort hat die stärkere Bedeutung? Kreuzen Sie an!

1.	☐ careful	☒ alert
2.	☐ friendly	☒ gracious
3.	☒ stunned	☐ surprised
4.	☒ skinny	☐ slim
5.	☒ shock	☐ scare
6.	☒ argue	☐ disagree
7.	☒ blurred	☐ unclear
8.	☐ small	☒ tiny
9.	☒ fog	☐ mist

Suddenly, Jessica noticed the lonely leafless tree which stood on its own overlooking the vast area.

"It was there, that's where I was!"

Inspector Hudson *nodded*. The tree was about 50 metres away from where Mr Smith's body was found.

"Was he found near here?" Jessica asked.

"Yes!"
She shivered at the thought that she had been so close to the murder.
"Did you see anything?"
"No, nothing at all… I was so… so frightened…Maybe if I had not run away, I could have helped…" Jessica said sadly.
"Believe me, it was the right thing to do," Inspector Hudson replied comfortingly.
Jessica was not so sure. She had a *guilty conscience*.
"Inspector Hudson!" suddenly shouted one of the policemen from down at the lake.
"Excuse me, I'll be back in a minute," the inspector said to Jessica.
He walked towards his colleagues. One of the divers was holding a long, dripping wet item in his hands. Jessica watched with great interest.
A crime detective – that might be a great and exciting job, she thought.
The diver handed the item over to Inspector Hudson. It was a *rifle*.
Inspector Hudson turned it in his hand and *scrutinized* it.
"Looks like a hunting *rifle*," he said to the diver.
The man *nodded*.
"Have it sent into the laboratory and see if it *matches* the *bullets* Martin Smith was shot with."
One of the dressed policemen took the *rifle*. Inspector Hudson walked back to Jessica.
"It's been a tough day," the inspector said. "I'll escort you home."
"Yes, it's so difficult to believe that Mr Smith is gone. Just the other day he was round for dinner and now he's gone, just like that – a click of the finger."
Inspector Hudson sighed, "Yes, death is the greatest tragedy."
The inspector paused. He was thinking about something.

"You were saying that Mr Smith was round for dinner?" he inquired.

"Yes, Mr Smith and Mr Lockwood were friends."

"I see," said Inspector Hudson thoughtfully.

"You do have an interesting job," Jessica said, changing the subject slightly.

"Do you think so?"

"Yes, your job is to get to the bottom of things, uncovering secrets."

Inspector Hudson smiled. He liked this girl. She was smart.

"If there is anything I can do to help, please let me know," Jessica *carried on*.

"Yes, but remember it's the police's job to catch the criminals," Inspector Hudson said kindly.

Jessica *nodded*, "I know, but I would love to see the murderer in jail before I leave England… Maybe a little help…"

"You are quite *stubborn*," Inspector Hudson laughed.

"That's what my Mum always says," she smiled.

"Well I'm sure she knows what she is talking about," replied the inspector.

ÜBUNG 17 !

Übung 17: Verwandeln Sie das Adjektiv in ein Adverb!

1. slow slowly
2. thoughtful thoughtfully
3. fast ~~quickly~~ fast
4. late late
5. safe safely
6. rough roughly

As Jessica *approached* the Lockwoods' house, she could already see Mr Lockwood looking anxiously out of the window. He seemed to be waiting for her.
Before Jessica could open the front door, Mr Lockwood had already opened it.
"Jessica, how are you?" he asked.
"I'm fine thanks, Mr Lockwood."
Jessica entered the house. Mr Lockwood closed the door behind her.
"I hope the inspector didn't *strain* you too much?"
"No, everything's fine."
"What did he want to know?"
"Not much. Just where I was when I heard the shots, if I saw anything or anybody, and so on. You know the usual questions the police always ask."
"So what did you tell him?"
"I couldn't tell him very much. I didn't see the murderer; all I heard were the shots."
"Yes, I see," said Mr Lockwood.
"Mr Lockwood, I'm a little tired. Would you mind if I lie down for a little while?"
"Oh yes, of course. Please excuse my *inquisition*. It's just… Well… Martin Smith was a friend and I just was anxious to know if there was any development in the case."
"No problem, Mr Lockwood, I understand. I'd like to see his killer behind bars as soon as possible, too."
"Thank you for your support, Jessica. I'm so sorry about this terrible experience," Mr Lockwood said.
"Well, it's not your fault," Jessica *shrugged*. "Call me if you need a hand with Kevin and Barbara.
She climbed the stairs. Mr Lockwood went into his *study*.

! ÜBUNG 18

Übung 18: Unterstreichen und verbessern Sie im folgenden Textabschnitt die acht falsch geschriebenen Wörter!

Jessica was lying in bed, but she could not sleap. Pictures of poor Mr Smith and how close she was to the murder scene *haunted* her. She *tosed* and turned in her bed. Jessica looked at the radio clock. It was just after midnight – the red digital numbers shining fiery into the darknes. Suddenly she heard a loud *bump*. The noise gave Jessica a fright. She listened into the darkness. Her nerves were not the best since the incedent out in the moor. Jessica got up, put on her dressing gown and opened her bedroom door. It was totally darc. Nobody apeared to be up. Just as she was about to go back to bed, there was another thump. This time it was a little quieter. It was coming from somewhere downstares. Jessica made her way carefully downstairs. Was there a burglar in the house? On her way to the kichen she noticed that a light was on in the cellar.

1. sleep
2. tossed
3. darkness
4. incident
5. dark
6. appeared
7. downstairs
8. kitchen

She noticed Kevin's baseball bat and picked it up. Jessica *descended* the stairs to the cellar. It was all *pitch-black* apart from the light coming from the washroom at the end of the corridor. Suddenly she saw a shadow pass beneath the door. Someone was in the washroom. Jessica gripped the baseball bat tightly and walked on carefully. She could hear the person moving things about. Jessica slowly opened the door, holding the bat ready to hit the intruder. Suddenly Mr Lockwood stepped out in front of her.

"My God, Jessica!" he exclaimed.
"Mr Lockwood, it's you?"
Mr Lockwood looked at the baseball bat which was still swung back in Jessica's hands. Jessica saw this.
"Oh, sorry!"
She put the bat down.
"What are you doing down here at this time of night?" Mr Lockwood said, still slightly shocked.
"Mr Lockwood… Sorry… I thought you were a burglar."
Mr Lockwood *calmed down* again.
"I guess this has all been a little too much," he sighed.
"Yes, I couldn't sleep…Then I heard this *bump*."
It was in that moment Jessica noticed to her *astonishment* the washing machine was going. She also saw his briefcase placed beside it. Why was he doing washing at this time of night? Jessica wondered. And apart from that, she had never seen him anywhere near the laundry room as long as she could remember. Mr Lockwood switched off the light in the laundry room and closed the door.
"I can't sleep either… What a dreadful day… Poor old Martin… Come on, I'll make as a cup of tea."

Übung 19: Setzen Sie ***to*** *oder* ***too*** *ein!*

1. Jessica was __too__ restless to sleep.
2. Mr Smith was on his way __to__ an appointment.
3. It's far __too__ misty __to__ go jogging.
4. Mr Lockwood had trouble sleeping __too__.
5. Inspector Hudson needs __to__ get more information.

ÜBUNG 19 !

Inspector Hudson was enjoying his tea and reading the morning newspaper in his office. He turned the page to find a large *obituary* for Martin Smith. It was from the bank: "So suddenly gone from us." it said.
A diplomatic way of saying murdered, Inspector Hudson thought.

There was a knock on his door.
"Come in!" he said.
Sergeant Wood entered.
"It's about the *rifle*. You were right. It's a hunting *rifle* – a Winchester Model 77 Semi Automatic 22 Caliber *Rifle*, to be precise, and it's normally used for hunting rabbits."
"Rabbits?" Inspector Hudson asked in a surprised voice. "I didn't know there were different weapons for different animals. That's news to me."
"Yes, you can get *rifles* for foxes, ducks, even *turkeys*," said Sergeant Wood, amused.
Inspector Hudson shook his head in *disbelief*.
"Does it *match* the *bullets*?"
"Yes, the *bullets* were fired from the *rifle*."
"Any fingerprints or DNA?"
"We're still working on that," answered the sergeant. "Since the *rifle* was wet, that part of the investigation might take a little longer."
"Very good, Sergeant."
"So where do we go from here?" Sergeant Wood asked.
"I think it might be a good idea to question Mr Lockwood next. Jessica, his au pair, told me that he was friends with Mr Smith. Perhaps he can help us out, because just now we're certainly not getting far."
The two policemen left the office.

Übung 20: Welche Synonyme gehören zusammen? Ordnen Sie zu!

1. ☐ hurry	a) shoot
2. ☐ honest	b) argue
3. ☐ pick	c) annoyed
4. ☐ assume	d) killer
5. ☐ murderer	e) suppose
6. ☐ fire	f) choose
7. ☐ quarrel	g) tactful
8. ☐ diplomatic	h) truthful
9. ☐ angry	i) rush
10. ☐ fiery	j) blazing
11. ☐ rifle	k) instant
12. ☐ moment	l) gun

Mr Lockwood agreed to talk to the police officers. He suggested that they meet at a small café around the corner from the bank. They shook hands and sat down at a table near the window.

“Thank you for meeting me here,” Mr Lockwood said. “I didn’t want to cause too much *commotion* at the bank. This is all getting too much for my employees.”

“Your employees?” Inspector Hudson asked.

“Yes, I’ve taken over the management of the bank… At least for just now, until things quieten down.”

“Jessica told me that you and Mr Smith were friends,” stated Inspector Hudson.

“Yes, we were well *acquainted*. Played squash together now and again and sometimes had each other round for dinner.”

“Did you notice anything strange in his behaviour lately?”

“No,” replied Mr Lockwood.

"Any enemies?" the sergeant asked.
"Not that I know of."
Sergeant Wood was writing all this down. Mr Lockwood looked thoughtfully at his hands.
"There is one thing, though… It's…"
Whatever Mr Lockwood wanted to tell the policemen, he seemed *reluctant* to do so.
"Yes?" asked Inspector Hudson
"It's just… I don't know if it's of any importance…"
"Everything is of importance to us, Mr Lockwood," Inspector Hudson said.
"Well, I know Martin was having an affair," said Mr Lockwood, forcing the words out.
"Do you know with whom?"
"Yes, it was Miss Olivia Anderson."
Sergeant Wood looked up from his writing pad. Inspector Hudson raised an eyebrow.
"Interesting," remarked the Inspector. "Very interesting. Are you absolutely sure?"
"I don't think for a moment that she has anything to do with the murder… It's just… I just thought…"
"You have been very helpful, Mr Lockwood, thank you," said Inspector Hudson, rising from his seat.
Sergeant Wood got up too.
"Can we *give you a lift* back to the bank, Sir?" he asked.
"No, thank you." Mr Lockwood answered. "I think I'll just finish my coffee."
The policemen said goodbye and exited the café. As they crossed the road to get to where their car was parked, Inspector Hudson looked back at the café. He saw Mr Lockwood sitting at the table, *stirring* his coffee – he looked slightly lost and sad.

Übung 21: Lesen Sie weiter und unterstreichen Sie jeweils die richtige Variante!

Inspector Hudson and Sergeant Wood (1.) were/where walking towards Olivia Anderson's flat. At the bank they were informed that Miss Anderson was on holiday that day. They were also (2.) said/told that she would most probably be (3.) in/at home. A woman came storming out of the flat entrance.
"There she is," said the Sergeant.
"And she's in quite a hurry if you ask me," replied Inspector Hudson.
Suddenly a man appeared from inside the flat also. He was about the same age (4.) as/like her, in his late twenties. The man stopped her. Miss Anderson tried to pull his arm away. He *grabbed* her and shook her.
"I think we've seen enough," Inspector Hudson said.
The policemen (5.) run/ran to the *threatened* woman's assistance. The man saw the policemen coming, let Miss Anderson go and ran away.
"Follow him, Sergeant, I'll take care of Miss Anderson," the inspector panted.
Sergeant Wood ran (6.) after/before the man, who *disappeared* around the corner.

Übung 22: Übersetzen Sie die folgenden Sätze!

1. Mr. Lockwood gab sein Einverständnis.

Mr. Lockwood agreed

2. Es gibt verschiedene Arten von Jagdgewehren.

There are different kinds of hunting rifles

Inspector Hudson took care

3. Mr. Smith war mit Mr Lockwood bekannt.

Mr. Smith was acquainted with Mr. Lock

4. Inspector Hudson kümmerte sich um Miss Anderson.

Inspector Hudson took care fore Miss Anderson

5. Sergeant Wood verfolgte den Verdächtigen.

Sergant Wood followed the suspect

Miss Anderson looked *pale* and was obviously very surprised to see the policemen.

"Are you okay?" Inspector Hudson asked her.

"Yes," she answered.

"Who was the man who was *threatening* you?"

"*Threatening*? We were just *quarrelling*. Michael, the man who just ran away, is my fiancé," she said *wearily*.

"What was the fight about?" the inspector asked.

"Nothing in particular, Michael can be a little bit jealous sometimes, that's all."

*Übung 23: Setzen Sie **many** oder **much** richtig ein!*

1. Inspector Hudson didn't have ________ time to solve the case.
2. Mr Lockwood could not tell them very ________ about Mr Smith's affair.
3. Mr Smith had ________ employees.
4. There were not ________ reasons for the murder.

5. Mr Lockwood's briefcase was __________ more bulky than usual.

6. There were not __________ clues.

7. Miss Anderson did not say very __________.

"Anyone in particular?" Inspector Hudson asked.
"No, sometimes it's enough to just look at another guy."
"I see," said Inspector Hudson.
Sergeant Wood turned up again.
"He got away, was *as fast as lightening*," the sergeant said, slightly out of breath.
"May we come in?" asked Inspector Hudson.
Miss Anderson looked at him *bewilderedly*.
"Into my house?"
"Yes," he answered.
"It's okay, I don't want to *press charges*."
"No, it's not about that. We want to talk to you about Martin Smith," Inspector Hudson said.
"Oh, I see," replied Miss Anderson uncomfortably. "Anything new?"
"Yes, I am afraid so," the inspector answered.
Without another word, Miss Anderson turned around and walked towards the flat entrance. The policemen followed her in.
"An affair with Martin Smith, you must be joking!" exclaimed Olivia Anderson.
The policemen and Miss Anderson were sitting in her kitchen, *steaming* cups of tea in front of them.
"We heard differently," Inspector Hudson said.
"Who told you, his wife?"
Inspector Hudson shook his head.
"What makes you think so?" he inquired.

"Because she was always jealous of me, she treated me like dirt whenever I crossed her *path*."

"You are saying then that you didn't have an affair with Martin Smith?" Sergeant Wood asked.

"Definitely not!" she insisted. "He was nearly double my age."

"Yes, but still attractive, charismatic and he also had a bit of money."

Olivia Anderson *tutted*.

"I don't believe this, now if you would please leave!"

"All we want to know…"

"Out!" Miss Anderson cried. "You have no right to say these things. Now get out!"

Sergeant Wood looked at his superior as if to ask how they should proceed now. Inspector Hudson signalled to him that he thought it better to leave for now. The policemen got up.

"Goodbye, Miss Anderson," Inspector Hudson said. "We are very sorry. We did not mean to *upset* you."

Miss Anderson just *glared at* them. Inspector Hudson and Sergeant Wood left Miss Anderson's apartment.

ÜBUNG 24 !

Übung 24: Beantworten Sie die Fragen zum Text!

1. What kind of hunting rifles can you buy?

2. Where does Jessica come from?

3. Where does Mr Lockwood work?

4. What kind of person is Miss Anderson's boyfriend?

....

5. Did Miss Anderson admit to having an affair with Mr Smith?

....

6. Why could Jessica not sleep?

....

7. Who ran away from the policemen?

....

"So what do you think?" asked Sergeant Wood as they walked along the street.
"I think that somebody is lying," the inspector answered.
"But why should Mr Lockwood lie to us?"
"I don't know. Maybe even Martin Smith lied to him."
"What do you mean?"
"Well, maybe he felt like showing off a little and told him some *fairytale* about having an affair."
"Do you really think so?"
"To be *honest*, I'm not sure. But it's always good to look at a case from all angles. Before jumping to conclusions, it's best to think every possibility through."
Sergeant Wood scratched his chin thoughtfully. "I guess you're right, Sir. Maybe even all three of them were lying."
"At the same time, it's also important to keep things simple," Inspector Hudson smiled. "Let's first of all assume that one of them was telling the truth and work our way from there."
Sergeant Wood *nodded* in agreement. Then his mobile rang.
"Hallo… yes, very good, we're on our way," the sergeant said.

He ended the conversation.
"Good news?" inquired Inspector Hudson.
"Yes, they've managed to *trace* some fingerprints on the *rifle* and are running them through the computer."
The policemen hurried back to the car.

! ÜBUNG 25

Übung 25: Welche der folgenden Aussagen sind wahr? Markieren Sie mit richtig ✔ oder falsch – !

1. The Lockwoods live near the moors. ☐
2. Jessica saw Mr Smith's murderer. ☐
3. Miss Anderson lives in a flat. ☐
4. Mrs Lockwood writes science books. ☐
5. They found the murder weapon in the woods. ☐
6. Mr Lockwood was writing letters in the middle of the night. ☐
7. Sergeant Wood caught Miss Anderson's boyfriend. ☐

Chapter 5: A Sad Day

Kevin was jumping all over Jessica's bed. Barbara was standing nearby *chuckling*. Jessica gradually came to.
"What's all this about?!" she said in a *pretend* annoyed voice.
"You've *slept in*," Kevin answered, laughing.
He was still jumping up and down on her bed. Jessica looked at the clock. It was nearly nine o'clock.
"But it's Saturday," she complained.
"Have you forgotten?" asked Barbara. "Mum and Dad are going out this morning."
Then Jessica remembered. It was the day of Mr Smith's funeral.

They did not want to take the children with them. Jessica was to look after them until they came back. She sat up. Outside she could hear car doors *slamming*. Jessica looked out of the window and saw Mr Lockwood's car drive onto the street. She stretched herself and *yawned*.

"All right, who's for some eggs!" she cried.

"I am, I am!" the children shouted at the same time.

Jessica got out of bed and led the children downstairs.

Übung 26: Übersetzen Sie und enträtseln Sie das Lösungswort!

1. Ei ☐ _ _
2. annehmen _ _ _ _ ☐ _
3. vielleicht ☐ _ _ _ _ _ _
4. verlassen ☐ _ _ _ _
5. ehrlich _ ☐ _ _ _ _
6. gähnen ☐ _ _ _
7. erinnern _ _ _ _ _ _ ☐ _
8. Stimme _ _ _ _ ☐

Lösung: _ _ _ _ _ _ _ _

Inspector Hudson was sitting in his office looking at a *file*. It was about a certain Michael Logan. He looked at the picture again. He knew that face. It was Olivia Anderson's boyfriend. His fingerprints were on the murder weapon. He already had a *police record*. *Assault and battery* were the main *offences*.

I wonder why Miss Anderson is going out with this man? the inspector thought.

Sergeant Wood entered his office.

"I've got some men together. We can leave whenever you want," he said.
"Let's bring him in," Inspector Hudson said.
He put down the police *file*.
"By the way," said the sergeant on his way out. "We couldn't find Martin Smith's mobile. It wasn't with his belongings and it wasn't in his *abandoned* car either."
"Then it has either been taken by the murderer or it has been lost on the moors. We should get some men to *comb* the crime scene later, it might still be lying about somewhere."
Sergeant Wood said he would do so and then they left the office together.

! ÜBUNG 27

Übung 27: Setzen Sie die richtigen Pronomen ein!
(me, him, mine, my, his (2x), her)

1. The inspector saw ___________ running away.
2. Excuse ___________!
3. To ___________ excitement they found fingerprints.
4. "The rifle does not belong to me, it isn't ___________."
5. They told ___________ she had slept in.
6. "That was _________ idea to make some eggs, not __________!"

Jessica could not read her magazine in peace. Kevin and Barbara were going totally crazy. They were jumping on the sofa and running around the *coffee table*.
"Kevin, Barbara, it's time we went out," she said.
"Ohhh, but we're having so much fun playing pirates that we

want to continue!" they protested.
"You can play pirates outside. It's a lot more fun."
"All right then," Barbara said.
"If we must," Kevin sighed.
The children hurried to the *cloakroom* to get their shoes and jackets. Not long after that, they were out on the moors. The children ran on in front of her. They were shouting and screaming, enjoying the fresh autumn air. While walking, Jessica could tell that she did not really like being out here anymore – it *gave her the creeps*. She was really looking forward to going home and getting away from this *uncanny* place. *It was a shame* because she really used to love being out here. The fresh clean air, the beautiful *scenery* – that is when the *mist* had cleared. Lost in thought, she hadn't been looking out for the children the last couple of minutes. When Jessica looked up, all of a sudden they were gone.
"Kevin? Barbara?" she called.
There was no answer. Where could they be? *Mist* was slowly starting to *creep* out of the ground. Jessica had to find them before it got thicker. She was very worried the children might fall into a wet, *muddy* part of the moor and sink in.
"Kevin, Barbara!" she cried.
There was still no answer. Jessica started running towards the area where she had last seen the children. However, they were nowhere in sight.
"Now, don't panic," Jessica tried to calm herself.
The *mist* was getting thicker. Then suddenly she heard something. It sounded like children's voices. Jessica ran in the direction of the voices. To her *relief,* they belonged to Kevin and Barbara. They were playing around in a *puddle*, *poking* about in it with *sticks*.
"There you are!" Jessica exclaimed. "You two shouldn't run away like that!"

Übung 28: Was ist gemeint? Finden Sie den passenden Begriff!

1. a place you hang jackets up: ______
2. a small pool of water: ______
3. left behind: ______
4. you can find it often under a tree: ______
5. a modern machine you can type on: ______
6. another word for landscape: ______
7. robbers at sea: ______

Suddenly Kevin cried out in surprise. He pushed something out of the *puddle* with his *stick*.

"I've found some *treasure*!" he shouted joyfully.

Jessica walked over to the *puddle*. Kevin lifted up his *treasure*.

"Look what I found. A mobile!" he exclaimed.

Kevin was holding a *muddy* item in his hand.

"Let me see?" Jessica asked.

"No, it's my *treasure*, I found it," protested Kevin.

"I just want to have a look, then I'll give it back to you."

He gave it to Jessica. It was a mobile phone. She looked at it. It was one of the very expensive and *flashy* ones. She had seen a model like this one somewhere before. However, she could not remember where. Jessica opened it. The display was blank. It was either switched off or damaged by the water. She had no means of checking who it belonged to. Jessica gave it back to Kevin.

"Come on, children, let's get home before this *mist* eats us all up!" Jessica made a ghostly noise. The children *screeched* with amusement and fear. They ran in the direction of the house.

Übung 29: Lesen Sie weiter und fügen Sie die Wörter in Klammern in die passenden Lücken ein!
(authoritarian, tapped, ram, remarked, collapsed, knocked)

ÜBUNG 29 !

Inspector Hudson (1.) __________ on Michael Logan's door several times. There was no answer. Suddenly Sergeant Wood saw a curtain move on the second floor. He (2.) __________ Inspector Hudson and showed him the curtain, which was still moving.

"Looks like our man is at home," he (3.) __________.

"This is the police, open up!" Inspector Hudson said in an (4.) __________ voice.

There was still no reply. He moved aside to let two policemen past. They had a kind of miniature *battering* (5.) __________ with them. They started to swing it at the door. After three hits the door (6.) __________ and the police ran into the house.

"Upstairs!" Sergeant Wood commanded.
The policemen ran upstairs. Suddenly Michael Logan appeared. He looked a little frightened.
"We only have a few questions," Inspector Hudson said.
"Questions?" asked. "What do you need half the London police force if you just have some questions? Get out of my house!" he *spat*.
"I'm afraid we can't," answered the inspector. "We have a *search warrant*."
Michael Logan looked at Inspector Hudson. Then he looked at the

other policeman. Suddenly, he tried to run past them to get down the stairs. However, Sergeant Wood managed to get hold of him. All of a sudden, Michael Logan pulled out a knife and *slashed* it at Sergeant Wood's arm.

"Argh!" he cried and let him go.

The other two policemen *grabbed* Michael Logan's arms and pulled him to the floor. The *suspect* was kicking and *swearing*. They took the knife from him. Inspector Hudson hurried over to Sergeant Wood. He was holding his hand.

"Are you all right?" he asked.

"Yes," the sergeant smiled *wearily*. "I might need a check for *rabies* though," he joked.

"We'll question him after he has *calmed down*," Inspector Hudson said.

Michael Logan was being *pinned down* by four men, still trying to fight them off. Inspector Hudson was glad when they eventually got the *handcuffs* on him.

ÜBUNG 30 !

Übung 30: Übersetzen Sie die Sätze im Konditional!

1. Inspector Hudson würde niemals ohne Sergeant Wood einen gefährlichen Verbrecher aufsuchen.

   Inspector Hudson would never call on a dangerous criminal without Sergeant Wood.

2. Sergeant Wood würde ungern zugeben, dass er dies auch nicht tun würde.

3. Michael Logan würde niemals mit einem Messer aus dem Haus gehen.

4. Inspector Hudson würde gerne den Mörder fassen.

5. Michael Logan würde am liebsten fliehen.

6. Sergeant Wood würde lieber keine Tollwut haben.

While the policemen were taking Michael Logan to the car, Inspector Hudson and Sergeant Wood looked around the house. They found a lot of literature on hunting.
Inspector Hudson picked up one of the books which were lying on the *coffee table*. He *flicked through* the pages. Suddenly, some photographs fell out. Sergeant Wood picked them up. He *whistled* and gave them to his superior. Inspector Hudson looked at them.
"It looks like Mr Lockwood was telling the truth," the inspector said, looking at the photographs.
They showed Olivia Anderson and Martin Smith kissing in a bar. Inspector Hudson put the photographs into his pocket.
"Jealousy seems to be the motive we're dealing with here," he said.
"Or a crime of passion, as the French would say," replied Sergeant Wood.
Inspector Hudson raised his eyebrow.
"That's very tolerant of them, isn't it?" the inspector said with a slight smile.

For sometime afterwards the inspector and the sergeant searched for Martin Smith's missing mobile phone. They could not find it.

! ÜBUNG 31

Übung 31: Ordnen Sie das passende Reflexivpronomen zu!

1. I could not make myself tell the truth.
2. You could not make ______________ tell the truth.
3. He could not make ______________ tell the truth.
4. She could not make ______________ tell the truth.
5. We could not make ______________ tell the truth.
6. You could not make ______________ tell the truth.
7. They could not make ______________ tell the truth.

Jessica, Mr and Mrs Lockwood and the children were sitting at the table having lunch. Mr and Mrs Lockwood were not long home and still dressed in black. The three adults had an aura of sadness around them. The children, of course, were too young to understand what was going on.
"How was the party?" asked Barbara.
"Party?" asked Mrs Lockwood.
"Yes, you and Daddy *are* all *dressed up*. You only do that on Saturdays when you go to a party."
The adults looked at each other slightly uneasily.
"I found some *treasure* out on the moor today!" Kevin *cut in*.
Everybody was *relieved* that the subject had been changed.
"That's great," Mr Lockwood said. "What kind of *treasure*?"
"A mobile, look!"

Übung 32: Setzen Sie die Verben in die richtige Zeitform ein!

ÜBUNG 32 !

Kevin (1. take) ________________ the mobile out of his pocket and gave it to his father. Mr Lockwood looked at it.

"Where did you (2. find) ______________ it?" Mrs Lockwood asked.

"Near the small lake."

"Any idea who it belongs to?" inquired Mr Lockwood, looking over at Jessica.

"No idea," she (3. *shrug*) __________________. "It was in a *puddle*. It's probably broken."

Mr Lockwood looked at the display.

"It looks like quite an expensive mobile," Mr Lockwood (4. say) __________________. "We should take it to the *lost property office*."

"But, Dad!" Kevin exclaimed. "I found it. It's mine!"

"No, it's not. It should be returned to its *rightful owner*," Mrs Lockwood said.

Kevin (5. start) __________________ to cry.

"Maybe we should give it to the inspector," Jessica said.

"The inspector, but why?" asked Mr Lockwood.

"Well, where Kevin found it was not too far away from… Well, you know…The place where…"

"It's just a silly old mobile. It's not Cluedo we're playing here. Let's leave the investigation up to the professionals, eh?" he (6. smile) ______________. "We don't want *harass* poor old Inspector Hudson with things like this, do we?"

Jessica (7. force) ______________ a smile.

"Who did he think he was talking to, a five year old?!" she (8. think) ______________.

"I'll take it to the *lost property office* first thing tomorrow, it's close to the bank," Mr Lockwood said. "And now Kevin, stop crying. I'll get you another one, okay?"
Kevin looked up, tears still running down his cheeks.
"Really?" he asked excitedly.
"Yes!"
"Great!" he *gasped*.
"And me, what do I get!" Barbara *cut in*.
"We'll get something nice for you, too, okay?"
Barbara *nodded* happily. Jessica excused herself and went to her room. She was still really tired.

Inspector Hudson was sitting across from Michael Logan in the interrogation room. The photographs of Olivia Anderson and Martin Smith were lying on the table. Sergeant Wood was standing by the door. His hand was bandaged. He was looking at Michael Logan with slight *displeasure*.
"Your fingerprints were on the murder weapon, you have these photographs, you're certainly not a *flimsy* lamb, you have been charged several times for *assault* – and you're still trying to tell me you have nothing to do with the murder?"
"No, I *swear*. As I told you, I was on a fishing trip."

"But you have no *witnesses*?"
Michael Logan shook his head.
"That's not really much good, is it?" said Inspector Hudson.

Übung 33: Setzen Sie, wenn nötig, ***a, an*** *oder* ***the*** *ein!*

ÜBUNG 33 !

1. Inspector Hudson travelled to Mr Logan's by __________ car.
2. __________ magazine had pictures in it.
3. Mr Logan made __________ big mistake by attacking Sergeant Wood.
4. Mr Lockwood came back form the funeral __________ hour ago.
5. Jessica got back out of __________ bed.
6. Jessica nearly lost __________ children.
7. If he is guilty, then Mr Logan will have to go to __________ prison.

"Where did you take the photographs?"
"I told you, I didn't take them. Someone sent me them."
"Do you still have the envelope they were in?"
"No," answered the *suspect* in *dismay*. "Look, I *swear* I didn't kill the man!"
"But you were *threatening* your girlfriend the other day. Did it have something to do with the photographs?" Inspector Hudson inquired.
Michael Logan paused. He was thinking.
"All right, all right… I asked her about the affair. I showed her the

photographs and she *denied* it. Then she ran out of her flat. And that's when you arrived on the scene. I mean, who wouldn't be jealous and angry – my own girlfriend having an affair with her boss!"

"And how do you explain your hunting *rifle* being found on the moors?"

"I have no idea, it was stolen. I didn't notice it until a couple of days ago."

"Do you know what I think?" asked the inspector *steadily*. "I think you were *suspicious*, so you followed Miss Anderson one evening and took the photographs. You were extremely angry and jealous. You managed to keep it *restrained* well enough to make sure that your girlfriend did not know you knew. Then you *lured* Mr Smith out to the moors and shot him. After a few days you could not stand her *deceit* any longer and confronted her with your jealousy."

"I *swear* I didn't kill the man, please believe me!" Michael Logan *pleaded*.

ÜBUNG 34 !

Übung 34: Übersetzen Sie folgende Sätze!

1. Seine Fingerabdrücke waren auf der Waffe.

2. Mr. Lockwood wollte das Telefon zum Fundbüro bringen.

3. Inspector Hudson glaubt Michael Logan nicht.

4. Michael Logan wusste von der Affäre.

5. Sergeant Wood trug einen Verband um seine Hand.

6. Der Verdächtige ist ein sehr eifersüchtiger Mann.

7. Michael Logan lockte Mr. Smith ins Moor.

Inspector Hudson shook his head.
"The evidence is too strong, how can I believe a word you say?"
Inspector Hudson turned towards Sergeant Wood.
"Sergeant!"
"My pleasure," he answered.
Sergeant Wood opened the door and called in a *constable*. The *constable* came in and took Michael Logan away in *handcuffs*.
"So what do you think?" the inspector asked Sergeant Wood, as soon as the *suspect* was out of the door.
"*Guilty*," he replied.
"Yes, I assume so, too. But he does seem rather *obstinate* about being innocent."
"But most of them do, don't they?"
"I guess so. I think we should question Miss Anderson once more. After all, she did lie to us."
The door opened again. Inspector Hudson's secretary put her head in.
"A Miss Jessica Langer is on the phone. She would like to talk to you."
"Did she say it was important?"
"No."
"Tell her I'll call her back in the morning."

"Will do," she replied.
Inspector Hudson looked at his watch.
"Enough for today, let's get a good night's sleep. Miss Anderson can wait until tomorrow."

ÜBUNG 35 !

Übung 35: Steigern Sie die folgenden Adjektive:

1. important	more important	most important
2. strong	______________	______________
3. much	______________	______________
4. many	______________	______________
5. helpful	______________	______________
6. clever	______________	______________

Chapter 6: Suspicions

Another night and again Jessica could not sleep. Every time she closed her eyes she saw thick *mist* and then heard the *deafening* shots. Mr Smith's face would appear in front of her inner eye. It was terrible… And then there was that mobile phone. She had seen it before. Who did it belong to? And why did Inspector Hudson not call back?
He doesn't take me very seriously, she thought.
Had the phone something to do with the murder of Mr Smith? She had to find out. Jessica got dressed and went downstairs. The mobile phone was no longer on the kitchen table where she had last

seen it. Where could Mr Lockwood have put it? She went into his *study* and eventually found it in one of his *drawers*. Jessica opened the display. It was on!

How could that be? she thought. Maybe it was on all the time and the display had a *malfunction* and is working again now. Or Mr Lockwood switched it on.

But how? Jessica had been quite certain that it was broken. She went into the menu and scrolled through the names. She found Mr Lockwood's number. Under "Office" she found the local bank's number. She *recognised* it because she sometimes had to call Mr Lockwood at work. Just the last three digits were different.

Could this be Mr Smith's mobile after all? she was thinking, biting her lip.

Übung 36: Ersetzen Sie das unterstrichene Wort durch das Gegenteil!

1. Jessica was <u>sleeping</u>. ____________

2. Inspector Hudson <u>closed</u> the door. ____________

3. Scotland Yard's office building is <u>huge</u>. ____________

4. Jessica was <u>upstairs</u>. ____________

5. Sergeant Wood <u>likes</u> Michael Logan. ____________

6. Mr Smith's mobile was <u>broken</u>. ____________

7. It is <u>easy</u> to get a hold of Inspector Hudson. ____________

Jessica found "Home". She walked over to one of the *shelves* and pulled out the *telephone directory*. She looked up Mr Smith's num-

ber and *compared* it with the number in the mobile. It *matched*! Suddenly she heard someone *approaching* the *study*. Jessica quickly put the phone directory back, put the mobile back in the drawer and switched off the desk light. She hid under the desk. The *study* door opened. She could see Mr Lockwood look in. Jessica held her breath. How *embarrassing* it would be if he found her *sneaking* about his *study* in the middle of the night. Mr Lockwood switched on the main light and walked in. Jessica sunk lower under the desk. His feet were now right in front of her face. Mr Lockwood walked to the other side of the desk. Jessica managed to pull her hand out of sight just in time. Mr Lockwood opened the drawer which *contained* the mobile phone. He took it out. Jessica was trying her best to breathe quietly. Then suddenly she felt the *urge* to sneeze.
Oh no! she thought.
Jessica *grabbed* her nose and held it tight. Mr Lockwood put the mobile in his pocket and closed the drawer again. He walked towards the door, closed it behind him and locked it from the outside.

ÜBUNG 37 !

Übung 37: Ergänzen Sie die If-Sätze mit ***will, would*** *oder* ***would have!***

1. If Jessica catches the murderer, she ____________ solve the case.
2. If Jessica caught the murderer, she ____________ solve the case.
3. If Jessica had caught the murderer, she ____________ solved the case.
4. Things ____________ get easier if Inspector Hudson was on the right track.

5. It ____________ get easier after Inspector Hudson has had a good night's sleep.

"Damn!" Jessica said.
She came out from under the desk.
So the mobile belongs to the murder victim, Jessica thought. But if so, what is Mr Lockwood planning to do with it?
And how was she supposed to get out of the office now? She searched the room. Maybe there was a *spare key* somewhere. Eventually she found the *spare key*. It was lying on one of the *shelves* near the door. She unlocked the door carefully and looked out cautiously. No one was in sight. Jessica *tiptoed* out of the *study*, closed the door quietly behind her and locked it.
I'll put the key back tomorrow, she thought.
Jessica *sneaked* back up to her bedroom.

Übung 38: Welche Wetterausdrücke gehören zusammen?

ÜBUNG 38 !

1. ☐	sun	a) lightening
2. ☐	cloud	b) clouds
3. ☐	fog	c) hurricane
4. ☐	thunder	d) mist
5. ☐	snow	e) clear sky
6. ☐	wind	f) blizzard
7. ☐	sky	g) rain

The next morning Olivia Anderson was sitting across from Inspector Hudson in his office. She was nervously *dragging* on her cigarette. She did not seem to be her usual *sophisticated* self at all. Miss Anderson looked tired and *worn out*.

"Okay, I *admit* it. Martin Smith and I were having an affair," she said.
In a way, she appeared to be *relieved* that she could *confess* to it. Being a policeman sometimes does have some *similarities* to being a priest, Inspector Hudson thought, amused.
"Why did you lie?" the inspector asked.
"Well, you saw my crazy boyfriend. I was afraid to *admit* it. Who knows what he might have done!"
"But he had the photographs."
"I know, but I was hoping to *convince* him that it was not what it looked like."
Inspector Hudson gave her a look of *disbelief*. Olivia Anderson sighed and put out her cigarette.

ÜBUNG 39

Übung 39: Wählen Sie die richtige Variante!

1. Jessica ________ hid from Mr Lockwood.
   a) ☐ scarcely
   b) ☐ immediately
   c) ☐ eventually

2. Normally Mr Lockwood was a ________ tempered person.
   a) ☐ well
   b) ☐ bad
   c) ☐ good

3. The mobile was ________ the drawer.
   a) ☐ at
   b) ☐ in
   c) ☐ on

4. Jessica came out from ________ the table after Mr Lockwood left the study.

a) ☐ under
b) ☐ over
c) ☐ down

5. In the dark Jessica had her eyes ________ open.

a) ☐ wide
b) ☐ large
c) ☐ greatly

6. Sergeant Wood ________ Michael Logan.

a) ☐ shadowed
b) ☐ trailed
c) ☐ followed

"I know it all sounds crazy. I'm about to *go around the bend* myself. I wanted to leave Michael long ago. He's jealous, often *ill-tempered* and he watches over me like a *hawk*. I was just afraid to leave. I thought he might *harm me*."
"And now he's *harmed* Martin Smith," Inspector Hudson remarked.
"Looks like it," she answered sadly.
"Do you believe him to be *capable* of murder?"
Olivia Anderson thought for a moment.
"Yes", she answered *briefly*.
"Did you love Martin Smith?"
Tears suddenly started to roll down her eyes. Miss Anderson bit her lip as if trying to *pull herself together*.
"Yes," she replied again in a *husky*, silent voice.
Inspector Hudson waited for Olivia Anderson to *calm down*. He

knew she was going to tell him more. All he had to do was to be patient.

"He wanted to leave his wife for me…We would have been so happy…"

Olivia Anderson started to cry again. The office door opened and the inspector's secretary looked in.

"Miss Jessica Langer is on the phone again," she announced.

Inspector Hudson just shook his head. Then the secretary noticed Miss Anderson crying. She excused herself and closed the door again.

ÜBUNG 40 !

*Übung 40: Setzen Sie **since, for** oder **ago** richtig ein!*

1. Miss Anderson started her affair a long time ________.
2. Michael Logan has been jealous ________ the beginning of their relationship.
3. Months ________ Inspector Hudson dealt with a similar case.
4. Mr Smith has been dead ________ two days.
5. Sergeant Wood has not been on holiday ________ July.

Jessica put the phone down.

You could probably get the Prime Minister on the phone easier than Inspector Hudson, she thought.

She had to talk to him. She wanted to tell him about the mobile phone and Mr Lockwood's strange behaviour. She could not quite believe he had anything to do with the murder, but, she did *feel* a little *uneasy* about the whole thing. Maybe there was another *explanation*, but she had to talk to the Inspector about it. Jessica also *recalled* the argument between Mr Lockwood and his boss the evening before his death. What had it been about? Then she remembered him doing his washing in the middle of the night. Jessica decided to go to the police station. On her way downstairs she *bumped* into Mr Lockwood. He was dressed and ready to go to work.

Übung 41: Welcher Satz enthält die richtige Übersetzung?

1. Jessica ging langsam die Treppe hinunter.
   a) ☐ Jessica gradually walked down the stairs.
   b) ☐ Jessica slowly walked down the stairs.

2. Sie war im Arbeitszimmer.
   a) ☐ She was on the study.
   b) ☐ She was in the study.

3. Jessica machte sich auf den Weg zurück zu ihrem Zimmer.
   a) ☐ Jessica headed back to her room.
   b) ☐ Jessica directed back to her room.

4. Olivia Anderson beruhigte sich nicht.
   a) ☐ Olivia Anderson didn't come down.
   b) ☐ Olivia Anderson didn't calm down.

5. Michael Logan verabscheute Nebenbuhler.
   a) ☐ Michael Logan disliked rivals.
   b) ☐ Michael Logan detested rivals.

6. Inspector Hudson ließ sie in Ruhe.

a) ☐ Inspector Hudson let her be.
b) ☐ Inspector Hudson let her go.

"Oh, Jessica, lucky I found you!" he said. "Have you seen the *spare key* from the *study*?"
Jessica paused. Her hand vaguely touched the pocket of her jeans. She could feel the key through the material.
"No, why, have you lost it?"
"Well, I am absolutely certain it was there before I locked the *study* last night and when I unlocked the door this morning, it was gone. It is very strange."
"I have no idea," Jessica lied.
Mr Lockwood looked at her *distrustfully*. It was just a second, but long enough to make Jessica *feel uneasy*.
"Are you sure?"
"Certain!" she answered, not taking her eyes off Mr Lockwood's.
"Oh, well," he *shrugged*. "Maybe I'm starting to get old."
Mr Lockwood smiled pleasantly. His short moment of *displeasure* was gone as though it had never existed. He realized Jessica had her jacket on.
"Are you on your way out, can I *give you a lift*?"
"No thank you, I was just going to get some fresh air before the children get home for lunch."
"Well, have a nice day, see you at dinner time."
Mr Lockwood turned around and walked back down the stairs. Jessica breathed out. I'm not a very good *liar*, she thought.

ÜBUNG 42 !

Übung 42: Vervollständigen Sie die Sätze mit ***good*** *oder* ***well***!

1. Detective Carlyle is a very ____________ policeman.

2. Sergeant Wood does his job really __________.

3. Michael Logan appears not to be __________ at lying.

4. Jessica is a __________ detective.

5. Mr Lockwood is always __________ dressed for work.

6. Mr Lockwood maybe thinks his brain cells are __________ for nothing.

7. Just as __________ Mr Lockwood did not see the key.

Inspector Hudson was walking through the corridor on his way back to his office. He had just escorted Olivia Anderson to the exit. Sergeant Wood saw his superior and hurried to catch up with him.
"We have new evidence against Michael Logan," the sergeant said.
"What have you got?" asked Inspector Hudson.
"I checked his mobile phone list with all the calls he had *recently* made."
"And?"
"And he called Martin Smith at 15:56. That must be around the same time he left the office."
"So Michael Logan was the mysterious phone caller."
"Well, we can't say 100 percent. However, the time he called him and the time Martin Smith left the office more or less *match*."
"I must say the evidence is very strong. Have you questioned Michael Logan about this?"
"Yes, he said that he had called him because of a business problem."
"Business problem?"
"Michael Logan works as a freelance consultant. He actually did some work for Martin Smith now and again."
"I thought Michael Logan was on a fishing trip?"

"He *claims* that while fishing, he had an idea on how to fix the problem. That's why he called him."
"It all *sounds* a bit *fishy* to me," remarked Inspector Hudson.
"Fishy – that's a good one," Sergeant Wood *smirked*.
"Looks like we've definitely got our man – inform the *prosecution*." Inspector Hudson ordered.
"My pleasure," answered Sergeant Wood.

ÜBUNG 43 !

Übung 43: Lesen Sie weiter und unterstreichen Sie die fünf inhaltlich nicht dazugehörenden Sätze!

Inspector Hudson was pleased. He felt really dull. It looked like they could *wrap up* the case. He entered his office and noticed a diary lying on the floor. The inspector picked it up, opened it and looked at the first page. Then he threw it out of the window. Olivia Anderson's name was written inside. It clearly belonged to Sergeant Wood. It must have fallen out of her bag when she took out her handkerchief. Olivia Anderson spoke to him in his dreams. Inspector Hudson would have it sent back to her. He placed it on his desk. Then he walked over to the window and looked out. The weather was not good at all. It looked like the sun might come out. Everything looked grey. He just stood there watching the world go by, when there was a knock on his door.

"Come in!" he said.
"You have a visitor, Sir," his secretary said.
"Yes?" he asked.
Inspector Hudson's secretary opened the door fully to let Jessica Langer in.
"Oh Miss Langer, please take a seat," Inspector Hudson said jovial-

ly moving his hand in the direction of the chair.
The secretary closed the door. Jessica sat down.
"I'm so sorry; I totally forgot to call you back. We've been very busy you know, please forgive me."
"No problem," Jessica replied.
"Now, how may I help you?" Inspector Hudson asked.
Jessica told him about the mobile phone and Mr Lockwood's strange behaviour.

Übung 44: Verwandeln Sie das Adverb in ein Adjektiv!

ÜBUNG 44 !

1. brutally brutal
2. far far
3. well good
4. highly high
5. low low
6. straight straight
7. only only

She also mentioned the argument she had overheard in the garden the evening before Martin Smith was killed. Inspector Hudson listened politely, *nodded* now and again and asked the *odd* question. However, for some reason, Jessica felt that he was not really all that interested in what she had to say.
"Do you not find that all very strange?" Jessica asked.
"Yes, it does sound slightly *peculiar*," the inspector answered. "And if the case were not *solved*, I would certainly look into it."

"*Solved*?" Jessica asked, astounded.

"Yes, it looks like we've got Mr Smith's murderer. But I must ask you to keep it to yourself for a while."

"Who was it?" Jessica asked.

"I can't tell you at the moment."

"Do I know him?"

"You are quite *persistent*, aren't you?" he laughed.

Jessica looked at him, slightly *sulky*.

"No, no, don't *get me wrong*. I think that's a great quality. You might make a great detective one day."

Jessica smiled.

ÜBUNG 45

Übung 45: Welche Synonyme gehören zusammen? Ordnen Sie zu!

1. ☐ delighted	a) unravel
2. ☐ strange	b) guest
3. ☐ solve	c) determined
4. ☐ visitor	d) peculiar
5. ☐ persistent	e) resentful
6. ☐ superior	f) pleased
7. ☐ sulky	g) boss

"And I'll tell you another thing. I'll phone Mr Lockwood and ask him to bring me the mobile phone. If it really belongs to Martin Smith, as you say, it is vital evidence. Who knows, maybe Mr Lockwood wanted to bring it in himself. He maybe just didn't say anything else about it because he did not want to cause too much *commotion*. You know, his child finding the evidence, something like that. Or maybe he hasn't even noticed it is working now."

"Yes," Jessica sighed. "All those things seem quite plausible.

Please don't tell him I was here telling you all this, he might feel *insulted*. And I'm still due my last month's pay."

Inspector Hudson *winked*.

"Don't worry, I'll think of something."

Jessica felt *relieved*. The office door opened again. It was Sergeant Wood.

"Can I have a quick word, it's important," he said.

"Of course," Inspector Hudson answered.

He got up and offered Jessica his hand.

"Thank you very much for your support and have a good journey home to Germany."

They shook hands.

"Thank you, Inspector," Jessica replied.

Then she left the office.

Übung 46: Welche Wörter gehören in die Lücken?
(commotion, secretary, rifle, mobile, evidence, insult)

ÜBUNG 46 !

1. A __________ assists her boss.

2. A __________ is a portable phone.

3. A __________ is a hunting weapon.

4. __________ is normally chaotic.

5. An __________ makes people sulky.

6. You need ________ to solve a case.

"Nice girl," Inspector Hudson said to the sergeant. "Now tell me, where's the fire?"

"This might sound a little irritating to you, but I've just been talking to a *witness* who saw Olivia Anderson's car parked in one of the moor car parks. It was not far away from where Martin Smith was shot."

Inspector Hudson could not hide his surprise.

"Maybe Michael Logan took his girlfriend's car on his so-called 'fishing trip'," Inspector Hudson said.

"I checked with Logan. He said he took his own car," the sergeant answered.

"He could be lying – maybe even trying to *set* his girlfriend *up*."

"I thought of that, Sir, so I called the bank. I found someone who could confirm that she had her car with her at the bank on the day of the murder."

"I see," said Inspector Hudson thoughtfully.

! ÜBUNG 47

Übung 47: Das englische Wort hat verschiedene Übersetzungsmöglichkeiten. Welche?

1. pretty ____________ ____________
2. just ____________ ____________
3. only ____________ ____________
4. well ____________ ____________
5. hand ____________ ____________

"And during the questioning I also found out something else."

"What?"

"I found out that Olivia Anderson left work shortly after Martin Smith."

Inspector Hudson said nothing. What could this all mean? Did it mean anything at all?
"They could be in it together," said the Sergeant.
"But why, I don't see any clear motives for that. She wanted to leave her boyfriend for him. And she's not in his *will* or anything."
"But why did she lie to us? She said she was in the office until six."
"She didn't actually say that, Sergeant. She made us assume she was in the office longer by telling us that Martin Smith did not return to the office the day he was killed."

Übung 48: Wie heißt das Simple Past der folgenden unregelmäßigen Verben?

1. lose ______________
2. let ______________
3. pay ______________
4. spend ______________
5. teach ______________
6. wear ______________
7. win ______________
8. shut ______________

"So where do we go from here?" asked Sergeant Wood.
"Good question. There is certainly something not quite right. I think we have two options."
"Which are?"
"Either Logan killed him, or Olivia Anderson killed him and has

set up her boyfriend. I don't think they're in it together."

Inspector Hudson looked at Olivia Anderson's diary lying on his desk. He picked it up and started to look through it. Something had been written in it on the day Martin Smith was murdered. Olivia Anderson had tried to *erase* it with *ink remover*. However, he could still see the *imprint* of what once was written there. Sergeant Wood looked over the inspector's shoulder. Inspector Hudson took a pencil and *scribbled* over the *imprint*. It read: "16:30 meet Martin".

"I think Miss Anderson *owes* us an *explanation*." Inspector Hudson said.

Sergeant Wood *nodded*.

"Oh, and before we leave, call Mr Lockwood. Jessica Langer *claimed* that his son found Martin Smith's mobile on the moors. Ask him if he would mind somebody coming round to *pick* it *up*."

"Yes, will do," said the sergeant and left the office.

! ÜBUNG 49

Übung 49: Wie lauten die Wörter in der richtigen Reihenfolge?

1. Anderson him killed up and Miss set him

Miss Anderson killed him and set him up.

2. quite not something right was

something was not quite right.

3. phone he caller mysterious was the

He was the mysterious phone caller.

4. it they in perhaps are together

perhaps ~~are~~ ~~they~~ they are in it together

5. opened in let to she door Jessica fully the

She opened the door fully to let Jessica in.

6. before shortly death called Logan his Mr Smith

Logan called Mr Smith shortly before his death

7. thinks behaving is Jessica Mr Lockwood strangely

Jessica thinks Mr Lockwood is behaving strangely

Chapter 7: Deceived

Olivia Anderson stood by the window. She was nervously smoking a cigarette. Inspector Hudson and Sergeant Wood were sitting on the *settee* looking over at her.

"I followed Martin the day he was murdered. He had not been himself lately. Martin refused to meet me several times… We used to meet secretly at the Lions Arms…" Olivia Anderson said with a sad, nostalgic smile.

"The hotel near the bank?" Inspector Hudson asked.

"Yes," she answered. "But he didn't want to see me that week… He seemed *preoccupied* with something else… He promised to meet me on Friday at 16:30. Our plan was to leave the office early separately and then meet at the Lions Arms. Then I saw him *receive* the phone call and leave the office in a rush without any *explanation*. Martin was not the type to do that sort of thing… I was worried..."

"Worried he may have another woman?" Inspector Hudson inquired.

"No, I was just *concerned*."

"*Concerned* about what?"

"About… Oh, I don't know!"

"So *concerned* that you followed him all the way to the moors?" the inspector asked.
Olivia Anderson *nodded*.
"Then what happened?"
"Well, I parked my car not far away from where he had parked his and followed him…"
Olivia Anderson paused. She was very nervous and lit another cigarette.
"Yes?" said Inspector Hudson.
"But it was extremely *misty*. Eventually I lost him… I tried to find him again, but was unsuccessful. I was worried that I would *lose my way*, I decided to head back to my car."
"Did you not find it strange that he was out on the moors in that weather?" Inspector Hudson asked.
"Yes, it did seem rather *odd*."
"And that was it? You walked back to your car and drove away?"
Olivia Anderson *dragged* deeply on her cigarette. She looked distantly out of the window.

ÜBUNG 50 !

Übung 50: Verneinen Sie die folgenden Sätze!

1. Olivia Anderson followed him to the moor.

Olivia Anderson didn't follow him to the moor.

2. The Lions Arms was near the bank.

....

3. Inspector Hudson knows who the murderer is.

....

4. It was very misty.

5. Sergeant Wood's men have found a clue.

"Miss Anderson?" said Inspector Hudson.
Olivia Anderson did not react.
"Miss Anderson?" the inspector repeated.
"I was almost at my car when I heard the shots."
"You heard the shots?" Inspector Hudson asked in a surprised voice.
"Yes," she replied.
"Why did you not tell us all this in the first place?"
"It wouldn't have brought Martin back to life, would it?" she answered, close to tears.

Übung 51: Welches Wort ist das „schwarze Schaf"?

ÜBUNG 51 !

1. follow, shadow, accompany, pursue
2. drag, leave, pull, heave
3. strong, feeble, muscular, brawny
4. close, distant, remote, far
5. fog, clear, mist, haze
6. sun, rain, snow, hailstones
7. time, clock, hands, numbers

Olivia Anderson was fighting back her tears. Inspector Hudson paused for a moment.
"But you are a vital *witness*, you might have helped us *solve* the

case," Inspector Hudson insisted calmly.
"Yes, or I might have ruined Martin's reputation. He was dead – what was the point!"
"He was murdered. Did you not want the murderer to be caught?"
"Of course I did, but I didn't see anybody or anything… Bad enough I could not help him. I often think if I had just not let him out of my sight… Perhaps… Perhaps he would still be alive…"

! ÜBUNG 52

Übung 52: Ordnen Sie die Buchstaben in Klammern zu einem sinnvollen Wort!

Olivia Anderson started to cry her (1. aehrt) ___________ out. The policemen were beginning to feel a little uncomfortable. Inspector Hudson (2. oostd) ___________ up.

"Perhaps you could come to the police station (3. twmorroo) ___________, when you're feeling a little better," he said.

Olivia Anderson did not look in his direction. She was still looking out of the window. She *nodded*. Sergeant Wood *got to his feet*.

"We'll let (4. uorsslvee) ___________ out," the sergeant said.

Olivia Anderson did not react. She was lost in thought. Sergeant Wood and Inspector Hudson walked to the living room door and (5. entw) ___________ out.

"What do you think?" asked Sergeant Wood, as they closed the front door behind them.

Inspector Hudson looked towards the living room window. Olivia Anderson was still staring out. She looked through them. Inspector Hudson *shrugged*.
"I don't know. She seems to be telling the truth. But there is something not quite right about the story. I'm just not sure what."

Übung 53: Welche der folgenden Aussagen sind wahr? Markieren Sie mit richtig ✔ oder falsch – !

ÜBUNG 53 !

1. The broken mobile was on when Jessica looked at it. ☐
2. Inspector Hudson reacted to Jessica's suspicions. ☐
3. Miss Anderson didn't hear shots. ☐
4. Inspector Hudson does not believe Miss Anderson. ☐
5. Miss Anderson didn't admit to having an affair. ☐
6. Mr Smith was acting normally. ☐
7. Mr Logan claimed to be at his grandmother's. ☐
8. Jessica attempted several times to get Hudson on the phone. ☐

Jessica could see the house in the distance. She was breathing heavily.
Don't stop now, just another five minutes to go, she thought.
It was the first time she had been out jogging since the shots on the moor. She wasn't really enjoying it and was glad to be back. Just before the garden gate, Jessica came to a halt. She opened it, walked along the *path* and unlocked the front door. Jessica walked past the living room. The children were watching a *cartoon* on the television. Mrs Lockwood was sitting nearby, typing the last chapter of her novel on her laptop.
I wonder how she does it, Jessica asked herself. I could never work with the children around.

Übung 54: Lesen Sie weiter und übersetzen Sie die Wörter in Klammern!

She walked upstairs and went to her (1. Zimmer) ______________.

Jessica froze the moment she opened the door. Her bed covers lay on the floor. One of the (2. Schreibtisch) ______________ *drawers* was open. Some of her clothes (3. lagen) ____________ on the floor.

"What on earth is going on?!" she exclaimed.

Who had *been amongst her* (4. Sachen) ______________? Jessica closed the door and walked into the room. She had just started to (5. aufheben) __________________ her clothes when suddenly the bedroom door (6. flog) _______________ open. Jessica got *the fright of her life* and dropped the clothes she was holding.

"Jessica, Jessica!" Kevin shouted (7. fröhlich) ________________.

"You're back! Do you want to play *snakes and ladders*?" he asked.

"Have you been in my room?" Jessica inquired.
"No," Kevin answered.
"And Barbara?"
"No, we never go into your room when you're out. Mummy doesn't allow it."
Jessica picked up the clothes she had dropped.
"Do you want to play a game of *snakes and ladders*, then?"
"No, not for the moment," replied Jessica, slightly more harshly than she had intended to.

Kevin looked *sulky*. Jessica saw his sad face and *instantly* felt sorry for him.
"I'll go for a shower and then we can have a game, okay?" she said softly.
"Great!" Kevin *beamed*.

Übung 55: Wählen Sie die richtige Variante aus!

ÜBUNG 55 !

1. Jessica was getting ________.
   a) ☐ nervous
   b) ☐ happy
   c) ☐ sad

2. Kevin ________ he had not been in her room.
   a) ☐ said
   b) ☐ told
   c) ☐ claimed

3. Jessica froze with ________.
   a) ☐ joy
   b) ☐ bliss
   c) ☐ fear

4. Somebody had been ________ her things.
   a) ☐ through
   b) ☐ over
   c) ☐ into

5. Mrs Lockwood was ________ to work with the kids around.
   a) ☐ contempt

b) ☐ happy
c) ☐ lucky

6. Kevin and Barbara wanted to ________.
   a) ☐ eat
   b) ☐ play
   c) ☐ drink

7. The children ________ the door open.
   a) ☐ smashed
   b) ☐ slammed
   c) ☐ threw

Sergeant Wood placed the mobile phone on Inspector Hudson's desk.
"Mr Lockwood brought the mobile phone round to the station, didn't even have to ask him for it," the sergeant said.
Inspector Hudson picked it up and looked at it. He opened it. The display was blank. The inspector hopelessly searched for the button to switch it on. Sergeant Wood smiled. Inspector Hudson was never very good when it came down to the technical side of things.
"Does it work?" Inspector Hudson asked, slightly *agitated*.
"No, it seems to be broken," answered Sergeant Wood.
"Strange, Miss Langer said it was switched on."
"The phone looks badly damaged. I can't imagine it worked."
"Miss Langer said it belonged to Martin Smith," the inspector remarked.
"Maybe she *is mistaken*," *shrugged* Sergeant Wood.
Inspector Hudson handed the mobile back to Sergeant Wood.
"Have it checked in the laboratory. Maybe we can save some of the information on it. And call Mrs Smith and ask her to describe her

late husband's mobile phone," he said.
Sergeant Wood *nodded* and left the office. Inspector Hudson stood up from his chair and walked to the window. He looked out. The sun was fighting against grey black clouds. A group of birds shot across the sky like a fast *sharp arrow*.

Übung 56: Bilden Sie die Pluralformen!

1. bus ____________________
2. plane ____________________
3. wish ____________________
4. tax ____________________
5. sandwich ____________________
6. pencil ____________________
7. foot ____________________
8. fish ____________________

Suddenly, the inspector's office door flew open. Sergeant Wood hurried in.
"Looks like he has got himself an alibi after all!" he *gasped*.
"Who, what do you mean?"
Sergeant Wood handed the documents he was holding over to his boss. It was a fine for *speeding*. The black and white photograph attached to the document showed Michael Logan.
"The photograph was taken just before five o'clock in the evening, minutes before Mr Smith was shot and about ten miles away," added the sergeant.

Inspector Hudson was thinking hard. Although he did not like to *admit* it, things were pointing in the direction of Olivia Anderson. Her car had been sighted and she had *admitted* to being out on the moors.

"Get a *search warrant* for Olivia Anderson's flat," Inspector Hudson said.

ÜBUNG 57 !

*Übung 57: Setzen Sie die richtige Zukunftsform **will** oder **going to** in die Lücken ein!*

1. We're in a hurry, I'm afraid you ________ have to take the mobile to the laboratory later.
2. Okay, I ________ take it there before I go home.
3. If we're lucky, this time tomorrow we ________ know more.
4. We're ________ to search Miss Anderson's flat today.
5. We're actually ________ take her to the police station.

Miss Anderson was being *guarded* by a *constable*. He was sitting on the *settee* reading a newspaper. The policeman's orders were not to let Olivia Anderson leave the living room. One could hear *drawers* being opened, doors being banged, items being moved about. She closed her eyes. It was very difficult to *bear* – strange people *poking* about one's belongings.

Inspector Hudson was scanning the incoming and outgoing emails in Olivia Anderson's email account on her laptop. There were several emails from Martin Smith. They were digital love letters; telling her how much he loved her; promising her that he would

soon leave his wife and save her from her brutal boyfriend. Sergeant Wood came over to him.
"Have you found anything interesting?" he asked.
"No, not yet," replied Inspector Hudson. "Has Miss Anderson given you any plausible answers yet?
"I'm afraid not," answered Sergeant Wood. "She told me she won't say anything without her lawyer."
Inspector Hudson scrolled down the emails. He could not find anything *suspicious*.
"I guess it's no problem to *delete* emails you don't want others to see," remarked Inspector Hudson.
"Have you looked in the *bin* which *contains* the *deleted* objects?" Sergeant Wood asked.
"*Bin*? What *bin*?" Inspector Hudson asked, looking down at the *wastepaper basket* under Miss Olivia's desk.
Sergeant Wood laughed.
"Do you mind?" he asked, bending towards the laptop.
"Not at all," the inspector said, moving out of the sergeant's way.
Sergeant Wood opened the "*deleted* objects" *file* and started to scroll through the *deleted* emails. Suddenly he *came across* something very interesting.
The email read: "Dear Olivia, it breaks my heart to do so, but I must end our relationship. I have come to the conclusion that I cannot go through with a divorce. I have decided to stay with my wife. You are so much younger than I am…"
"Looks like Miss Anderson forgot to *delete* this email entirely," Sergeant Wood remarked.
"Yes, lucky for us," said Inspector Hudson.
"It was sent the day before Martin Smith was murdered," the sergeant said.
"I guess Miss Anderson was *leading us astray* all the time. She told

us that Martin Smith wanted to leave his wife for her, remember?" said the inspector. Sergeant Wood *nodded*.

ÜBUNG 58

! *Übung 58: Ordnen Sie die Wörter auf der rechten Seite den Begriffen auf der linken zu!*

1. ☐ plausible	a) chance, fluke, accident
2. ☐ unforeseen	b) lure, attract, entice
3. ☐ guess	c) probable, likely, possible
4. ☐ tempt	d) bright, smart, intelligent
5. ☐ clever	e) separate, split, break up
6. ☐ divorce	f) make-up, play, make-believe
7. ☐ coincidence	g) presume, assume, estimate
8. ☐ pretend	h) unexpected, surprising, sudden

"Now we have her motive. She probably *lured* Martin Smith out to the moors, telling him they must talk in private. She wanted to talk him out of leaving her. He said no. Then she shot him with her boyfriend's *rifle*."

"But it was very careless of her to leave the bank shortly after him and to also park her car near the moor, was it not?" the sergeant asked.

"Yes, it was *indeed*," answered Inspector Hudson. "However, she did very well at *setting up* her boyfriend. If it were not for the *coincidence* that he was caught *speeding*, he would have probably been charged with the murder," said the inspector.

"She certainly had us *fooled*. But what about the photographs we found at Michael Logan's house?" Sergeant Wood asked

"Perhaps she had them done by a private detective, for example, and then sent them to him. She knew it would make him awfully jealous and more *suspicious*," replied Inspector Hudson. "Let's take her in for further questioning," he continued.

Übung 59: Setzen Sie das richtige Adjektiv ein!
(good, clever, helpful, dangerous, funny, lucky)

ÜBUNG 59 !

1. That was a very ____________ plan.
2. Finding the email was ____________.
3. Inspector Hudson is not a very ____________ computer expert.
4. Miss Anderson appeared to be a ____________ woman.
5. Miss Anderson was not amused; she did not think the email was very ____________.
6. It was ____________ that she did not delete the email.

A *constable* escorted Olivia Anderson to a police car. She did not resist at all and did not say a word. She had actually hardly spoken since the police had arrived at her house. Olivia Anderson looked sad and tired. Her beautiful face *was scared* by *sorrow*.
"Very tragic," Sergeant Wood said to the inspector, who was watching the whole procedure.

Übung 60: Enträtseln Sie die fünf Begriffe, die man stellvertretend für ***beautiful*** *sagen könnte!*

ÜBUNG 60 !

1. omenadhs ____________
2. nnsutign ____________

3. trativecta ______________

4. rgeouogs ______________

5. doog-lkooing ______________

6. eyrptt ______________

The *constable* opened the car's back door. Olivia Anderson got in. The policemen closed the door, went to the driver's side, got in and drove away. The car was just gone, when suddenly a bright red sports car shot round the corner.

"What on earth…!" exclaimed Sergeant Wood.

The car braked right in front of them. The *tyres* squeaked. There was a distinct smell of burning *rubber* in the air.

Inspector Hudson smiled. Sergeant Wood was still a little shocked. Then suddenly he also realised who it was. An elegant and attractive woman got out of the car. It was the insurance agent Elvira Elliot. She smiled at the policemen.

"This can't be a *coincidence*," remarked Inspector Hudson in a friendly tone.

"I don't believe in *coincidences*, Inspector, do you?" Elvira Elliot smiled.

Inspector Hudson laughed. Sergeant Wood smiled slightly *awkwardly*. This beautiful and confident woman always made him *feel* a little *uneasy*.

"How can we help you?" the inspector asked.

"You're working on the Smith murder just now, right?" she asked.

"Yes," replied Inspector Hudson. "But murder is not usually your cup of tea."

"But money is. And it appears that a lot of it has been going missing lately in the bank where Martin Smith worked."

Inspector Hudson and Sergeant Wood looked surprised to hear this.

Übung 61: Lesen Sie weiter und unterstreichen Sie die Synonyme der Wörter in Klammern!
(1. precisely, 2. examine, 3. rejected, 4. ardour, 5. proof, 6. asked)

ÜBUNG 61

"*Embezzlement*?" asked the inspector.
"Exactly," replied Elvira Elliot. "My insurance company wants me to *investigate* it. If the money doesn't turn up again, it's going to cost them millions."
"Millions?" Sergeant Wood asked.
"Yes," she answered.
The sergeant *whistled*.
"How is your investigation coming along? I hear you have a *suspect*," Elvira Elliot said.
"It looks more like *spurned love*," Inspector Hudson replied.
"A crime of passion, you think?" Elvira Elliot remarked.
"Looks like it," Sergeant Wood replied.
"Come on!" she joked. "We're not in France. We British don't kill for love, it's not our style."
"The evidence is very strong," the inspector argued.
"Has the *suspect admitted* anything yet?"
"No! Do you think there might be a connection between Martin Smith's death and the *embezzlement*?" inquired Inspector Hudson.
Elvira Elliot *nodded*. Inspector Hudson and Sergeant Wood looked at each other.

Übung 62: Welches Wort ist das „schwarze Schaf"?

ÜBUNG 62

1. find, discover, ascertain, mislay
2. suspect, gun, murder, victim
3. worry, fret, exasperate, wish

4. right, wrong, incorrect, false
5. innocent, guilty, guiltless, blameless
6. believe, trust, doubt, rely
7. odd, weird, normal, strange
8. steal, pinch, give, take

"This certainly adds a new *twist* to the case," said Inspector Hudson. "There is of course one other possibility," he *carried on*.

"What could that be?" Miss Elliot asked.

"The *embezzlement* and the murder are not connected," the inspector argued.

"That is a possibility, I agree," replied Elvira Elliot.

"Does the bank have any idea who is behind all of this?" asked Inspector Hudson.

"No, I'm afraid not. However, the money was *embezzled* about a week before Martin Smith's death."

"Maybe he had something to do with it all. It might be some kind of Mafia thing. And he got himself caught up in something that had to end up bad for him," said the sergeant.

"I'm not quite sure," Inspector Hudson said. "What about Olivia Anderson?"

"Olivia Anderson?" Elvira Elliot inquired.

"Our main *suspect*," the inspector informed her.

"Perhaps she killed for the money," said the insurance agent.

"Perhaps, but I don't really think so," Inspector Hudson replied. He was thinking hard again, lost in thought.

"Best thing is you look further into the money transactions, try and find out who took the money and where it went."

"Thanks for telling me how to do my job," Elvira Elliot remarked, with a flirtatious smile.

Inspector Hudson ignored her comment.

Übung 63: Bilden Sie die Pluralformen!

1. policeman ....
2. smile ....
3. sheep ....
4. scarf ....
5. wife ....
6. half ....
7. witness ....
8. lady ....
9. tooth ....

"In the meantime we'll question Olivia Anderson and maybe ask Martin Smith's wife a couple of questions," he finished.
"Ah, a good thing that you mention it, Inspector, I nearly forgot because of all the *commotion*. Mrs Smith told me that her *late husband* owned a mobile phone like the one found in the moors."
"Good, have you handed it into the *lab*?"
"Yes," replied the sergeant. "If we can restore some information like text or voicemail messages, that might be very helpful," the sergeant said.
"Okay then, let's get back to the police station," Inspector Hudson said.
"Can I *give anybody a lift*?" asked Elvira Elliot.
"Oh, no thanks!" answered the inspector. The very thought of being a victim of Miss Elliot's driving tactics made him *feel uneasy*.
"And you, Sergeant?" she inquired.

"Oh… Erm… Well, maybe another time," he smiled *awkwardly*.
"Okay, then. I'll see you guys later," she said.
Elvira Elliot got into her car and shot off like a rocket.

ÜBUNG 64

Übung 64: Enträtseln Sie die folgenden Definitionen!

1. To misuse funds: ______________ (zemezleb).
2. Great disturbance or motion: ______________ (ooomctimn)
3. A place where things are analyzed: ______________ (balorytora)
4. You can invest in them: ______________ (nufsd)
5. A weapon or space vehicle: ______________ (ktcreo)
6. Happy about something: ______________ (lagd)
7. Related or joined together: ______________ (dncoentec)
8. Something that happens by chance: ______________ (ecnedic-nioc)

The two policemen looked at each other. Inspector Hudson *shrugged*.
"I'm glad we *gave* that *a miss*," Sergeant Wood said.
They walked towards the police car.
"Nice woman, though," remarked the sergeant, before opening the car door.

Inspector Hudson just raised his eyebrow – expressing a little surprise at the remark Sergeant Wood had made.
Then he got into the car.

Übung 65: Welche Gegenteile gehören zusammen? Ordnen Sie zu!

ÜBUNG 65 !

1. ☐	deadly	a) unfriendly
2. ☐	motion	b) drop
3. ☐	nice	c) somebody
4. ☐	miss	d) lower
5. ☐	nobody	e) stillness
6. ☐	lift	f) hit
7. ☐	raise	g) harmless

Chapter 8: Deadly Moonlight

It was late in the evening. The police station was quiet and empty. Elvira Elliot was sitting on the *edge* of Inspector Hudson's desk. Inspector Hudson was *brooding over* an endless *file* of numbers. His *forehead* was *wrinkled*. He was obviously thinking hard about something. Elvira Elliot was watching him. She smiled.

"Is everything all right?" she asked.

"Yes, yes," Inspector Hudson replied *casually*.

Elvira Elliot was not *convinced*.

"If you want me to explain anything…" she said.

"No, no, everything is fine, thank you," answered the inspector.

Elvira Elliot looked at her fingernails.

They could do with a manicure, she thought.

Inspector Hudson put the documents aside.

"So what do you think?" Elvira Elliot asked.

"A lot of numbers, that's what I think," Inspector Hudson replied.

"But did you notice the *pattern*?"

"*Pattern*?"

Elvira Elliot *tutted* and picked up the paper *files*.

"Somebody appears to be *diverting* small *amounts* of money from the bank from different *funds* which made a profit. However, the person has done it *on* such *a big scale* that the money soon *adds up*."

"I see," said Inspector Hudson.

"And to hide this procedure, the person has invented different companies and investors that do not exist."

"They do not exist," said the inspector slightly puzzled. "Can you *figure out* by analysing the accounts who *diverted* the money?"

"Not exactly, but most of the *funds* in question are in Martin Smith's area of responsibility."

"Do you think he was behind all this?"

"It could well be. He had easy access to all of his clients' information. And as the bank manager, he had access to certain accounts, procedures and dealings which nobody else had.

"I wonder why he would do such a thing."

"Maybe he had money problems."

"His wife doesn't seem to know about anything of the sort. I mean, soon after his death, his *alleged* debt was sure to be uncovered," remarked Inspector Hudson.

"Perhaps there's still something that hasn't *cropped up* yet," said Elvira Elliot.

ÜBUNG 66

Übung 66: Lesen Sie weiter und setzen Sie das richtige Wort ein!
(remain, case, betrayed, accomplice, campaign, work, embezzled)

"Okay, let's say Martin Smith (1.) ____________ the money and his murder is connected to it," said Inspector Hudson. "And he wasn't in it alone."

"Yes, that's often the (2.) ____________," Elvira Elliot agreed.

"So he had someone in it with him. The (3.) ____________ got greedy, wanted the money for himself and killed him."

"Possible," remarked the insurance agent.

"Would the accomplice have had to (4.) ____________ in the bank, too?" Inspector Hudson asked.

"Well it does make the whole (5.) ____________ much easier. One can cover things up easier if both work in the bank," Elvira Elliot replied.

"That would mean that Olivia Anderson would still (6.) ____________ our main *suspect*. She was his *mistress*, he got her to help him to *embezzle* the money, he gets what he wants and then he *dumps* her. Olivia Anderson feels (7.) ____________ on both levels and decides to kill him."

"Sounds like good crime drama to me," remarked Elvira Elliot.
"I could do with a little less of it," Inspector Hudson sighed. "It looks like Olivia Anderson is more than just a *suspect* now."
"Has she said anything yet?"
"No, she has not spoken a word."
"Silence is close to *confession*," Elvira Elliot commented.
"Shakespeare?"
"No," she laughed. "Elvira Elliot!"
Inspector Hudson laughed too. "Have you been in contact with Mr Lockwood, the new bank manager?" the inspector asked.

"Yes, he has been very cooperative. He's *given me free rein* to *investigate* in the bank – a very nice man actually, always helpful and *polite*."

Inspector Hudson *nodded*. He looked at his watch and *yawned*.

"It's late again," he said. "Tomorrow we'll interview Martin Smith's wife. And hopefully Miss Anderson will at least talk to us.

! ÜBUNG 67

Übung 67: Setzen Sie das passende Wort in die Lücken ein!
(through, to (2x), up (2x), under, close)

1. Jessica couldn't get ____________ to Inspector Hudson.
2. Silence is ____________ to confession.
3. Mr Smith died ____________ mysterious circumstances.
4. The policemen started ____________ follow him.
5. Miss Elliot caught ____________ with the policemen.
6. He hopes Miss Anderson will talk ____________ them.
7. Miss Elliot picked ____________ the files.

It was very late at night. Jessica was restless. *Aggravating* thoughts were running through her head. Who had been in her bedroom and why? Had Mr Lockwood been looking for his key, which she had completely forgotten to put back? She got up and went to her desk. Jessica wanted to write her boyfriend a letter – that might *distract* her, she thought. Jessica took a pen und *spread out* a sheet of paper before her. Just as she was about to start to write, she heard the front door open. She listened. Then Jessica walked to her door and opened it slightly.

Übung 68: Übersetzen Sie!

1. Jessica war unruhig.

2. Morgen will Inspector Hudson mit Miss Anderson reden.

3. Mr. Smith hatte womöglich einen Komplizen.

4. Jessica hatte unangenehme Gedanken.

5. Mr. Smith hatte Zugang zu besonderen Konten.

6. Es ist einfacher die Sache zu zweit durchzuziehen.

7. Miss Anderson bleibt die Hauptverdächtige.

She could see Mr Lockwood going downstairs. He was carrying a *pile* of papers and walking in the direction of his *study*. Jessica wondered why he was home so late. She was also surprised to see him with such a large stack of documents. Did he really have that much work to do? Jessica could not *get rid of* the feeling that something *weird* was going on. Mr Lockwood had been behaving very strangely *recently*. Did Mrs Lockwood not notice? On the other hand, she lived in such a dream world, always inventing new stories for her latest novel.

ÜBUNG 69 !

Übung 69: Beantworten Sie die Fragen zum Text!

1. Could Jessica sleep?

2. What was Mr Lockwood carrying?

3. Why could Jessica not sleep?

4. Did Mrs Lockwood notice that her husband was acting strangely?

5. What does Mrs Lockwood want to do for a living?

6. Did Jessica call her boyfriend?

7. Did Mr Lockwood go straight to the bathroom when he got home?

She probably wouldn't see a Jumbo land in her garden if she was working on her book at the same time, Jessica thought.
Jessica observed what was going on from behind her bedroom door. Suddenly Mr Lockwood came back. He switched off the lights downstairs and came upstairs. Jessica closed her door carefully. She listened. Mr Lockwood went into the bathroom. After he

had finished, he went into his bedroom and closed the door. After waiting for a couple of minutes, Jessica opened her door – *the coast was clear*. Jessica *sneaked* downstairs. It was full moon. This made it easy for her to *make out* the outlines of the stairs. With wide eyes she made her way downstairs. Since she was only wearing socks, she made very little noise. Suddenly one of the *stair boards* creaked loudly. She froze, *straining her ears* trying to hear anything *stir* upstairs. Everything was silent. Jessica moved on and thankfully reached the bottom step. Then she *tiptoed* towards the *study*. It did not surprise her to find it locked. She took the *spare key* out of her dressing gown pocket and unlocked the door. Jessica entered the *study*. The moon cast *pale* light over the *bookshelves*, creating *eerie* shadows that looked like ugly *goblins* with *sharp* noses and deadly horns. On the desk she saw the *pile* of papers. Jessica walked over to them and switched on the desk light. She took some sheets from the *pile* and looked through them. They where full of transactions. It appeared that Mr Lockwood had been transferring large *amounts* of money from the bank to a private account in Switzerland. All of a sudden the *study* door opened. Mr Lockwood came in. He did not say a word, just stared at Jessica with great *displeasure*.

Übung 70: Übersetzen Sie und enträtseln Sie das Lösungswort!

1. Stapel _ _ _ □
2. Summe _ □ _ _ _ _
3. Ehemann _ _ _ □ _ _ _
4. schulden _ _ □
5. Schweiz _ _ _ _ □ _ _ _ _ _ _
6. schwindelig _ _ □ _ _

7. Türschloss ☐ _ _ _
8. Geliebte _ _ _ _ _ ☐ _ _
9. Abdruck _ ☐ _ _ _ _ _
10. schreiben _ _ _ _ ☐
11. Drache _ _ _ _ _ ☐
12. Konto _ _ _ _ _ _ ☐

Lösung: _ _ _ _ _ _ _ _ _ _ _ _

"Mr Lockwood…Erm…I was…" Jessica *stammered*.
"Have you being looking at my account sheets?"
Jessica put the sheets she was holding in her hands back on the *pile*.
"No… Well, maybe a little… But I don't understand a lot about these things anyway," Jessica replied.
"Yes, I've had a lot of work to do *recently*."
"I think I'll just go back to bed then," Jessica said.
She walked towards the open door, but as she *approached* it Mr Lockwood closed it.
"I'm afraid it's just not quite as simple as that," Mr Lockwood said.
Jessica looked at him. She was getting fed up with this cat and mouse game, especially because she was the mouse this time around.
"Mr Lockwood," she said in an authoritarian voice. "I would like to go to bed now!"
He did not *budge*.

ÜBUNG 71

Übung 71: Übersetzen Sie die Imperative!

1. Jetzt! ______________________

2. Mache es richtig! ______________________

3. Bleib da! ______________________

4. Hinsetzen! ______________________

5. Genug davon! ______________________

6. Tu es nicht! ______________________

7. Kommen Sie her! ______________________

8. Nicht laufen! ______________________

9. Hören Sie damit auf! ______________________

10. Nicht jetzt! ______________________

"Jessica, I wish you were not so *nosy*," he said *regretfully*.
Jessica tried to walk past him to get to the door. Mr Lockwood stood in her way.
"If you don't let me out, I'll scream!" Jessica *threatened*.
Mr Lockwood pulled out a gun. Jessica stared at the weapon in horror.
"I would think twice about that if I were you," he said calmly.
He pointed with the gun towards the veranda door.
"This way, please."
Jessica did not move.
"I mean it!" Mr Lockwood said in an annoyed voice.
She turned around and walked in the direction of the veranda door. He made her open the door and then they stepped into the cold night. A sudden shadow crossed over the moonlight. Jessica looked up. A dark cloud had *swallowed* the moon. That can't be a good omen, she thought.
"Move on!" Mr Lockwood ordered.

Jessica glanced at her feet. She had no shoes on. Her feet were cold already. Then she started to put one leg in front of the other. It was not easy, as her legs were shaking with fear.

ÜBUNG 72 !

Übung 72: Vervollständigen Sie die Relativsätze!
(who (2x), that, whose, which)

1. Mr Lockwood, ________ worked in a bank, was a very deceitful man.
2. Jessica, _______ life was in danger, was very frightened.
3. She was trapped in the study _______ belonged to Mr Lockwood.
4. Mrs Lockwood, _________ was in bed, didn't hear a thing.
5. The Lions Arms, _______ usually opens on Mondays, was closed.

Mr Lockwood was walking a few steps behind Jessica. He was pointing the gun at her the whole time. They were following the *path* Jessica often jogged on. The car park for *ramblers* and the road leading to town were not far away. The cold, *damp mist* was *clinging* to her body like a heavy wet cloth. She had to flee now, before it was too late.
"Can we not talk this over?" Jessica asked.
"I think we've done enough talking," replied Mr Lockwood.
Jessica walked on. Her feet were very *sore*. She kept on scraping them on stones and branches.
"You're never going to get away with this!" Jessica said.
"I think my chances are fairly good. The police have already charged someone with Martin's murder and only you know about

the transactions. Now the game is over!"
"But they'll come looking for me. You *don't stand a chance…*"
"Silence," Mr Lockwood *hissed*. "Do you think this is easy for me? But I'm not really worried. I can already see the newspaper headline: 'Young German au pair tragically lost on deadly Moor'. You wouldn't be the first one to go missing out here… Now hurry along, so we can get it over with."
It was now or never, Jessica thought. It was at that moment that Jessica *recognised* the *spot* where she had left the trail and slid on the wet grass a couple of nights ago. What were her chances? If she was fast enough, she could *disappear* down the *slope* into the *mist*. He's probably a bad *marksman* anyway, Jessica thought, trying to *encourage* herself.

Übung 73: Welche Bedeutung haben folgende Sätze? Kreuzen Sie an!

ÜBUNG 73 !

1. Can we talk this over?
   a) ☐ Let's talk until one of us gives up.
   b) ☐ Let's talk the whole thing through.
   c) ☐ Let's not talk at all.

2. Her chances were fairly good.
   a) ☐ She had no chance.
   b) ☐ She liked good chances.
   c) ☐ She could make it.

3. To think twice about something.
   a) ☐ to think something over.
   b) ☐ to think double as much.

c) ☐ to stop thinking about something.

4. They managed to restore information.
   a) ☐ They run an information store.
   b) ☐ They had no chance ever getting the information.
   c) ☐ They were successful at regaining information.

5. Mr Lockwood is bad company.
   a) ☐ He's dangerous.
   b) ☐ He works for an appalling firm.
   c) ☐ He loathes good company.

Jessica *took a deep breath*, counted to three and then without any warning she started to sprint. Once she got going she was *convinced* that nothing could stop her. It took Mr Lockwood a second or two to realise what was going on, but then he pointed the gun in her direction and fired. As she stumbled over a rock, a *bullet* just missed her head by a few inches. The *mist* was very thick and it was hard for her to find her way. Mr Lockwood was close behind. She could hear his footsteps on the ground. He fired another shot. Jessica ducked instinctively, feeling stupid about it at the same time, because she had no idea from where the *bullet* was coming from. Jessica looked back over her shoulder, flicking a glance at Mr Lockwood. She did not notice a *hollow* in the ground. She *sprained* her ankle and lost balance. Jessica fell flat on the floor. She looked up. Mr Lockwood was nowhere in sight, but she could hear his steps. Jessica quickly got back on her feet, but she had problems running, her foot *hurt like mad*. Nevertheless, she tried to move on as fast as she could. Jessica could see the road in the distance. Her foot was getting worse. She looked around again. Mr Lockwood was very close now. Jessica felt another *sharp* pain in her foot.

Übung 74: Welche Begriffe werden gesucht, die sich auf eine Mordermittlung beziehen?

ÜBUNG 74 !

1. The person who is thought to have committed a crime.

____

2. The person who has been murdered.

____

3. The general word used for a person who is not guilty.

____

4. The general name for the process involved in solving a crime.

____

5. The place a criminal goes to when he has been convicted.

____

Oh God, I'm not going to make it! she thought.
Anger and physical pain shot through her body. Her eyes flooded with tears. She would not give up; she had to reach the road. It was her only hope. Jessica clenched her teeth and started to run faster. The pain was almost *unbearable*. Mr Lockwood was getting closer. Why has he stopped shooting? Jessica wondered. Maybe we are too close to the road.

ÜBUNG 75 !

Übung 75: Setzen Sie die Verben in die richtige Zeitform ein!

Jessica (1. is) ____________ actually very close to the road by now.

Mr Lockwood was still close behind her. While (2. run) __________, he was trying to reload his gun, but he was having difficulty doing both things at the same time. He (3. have) __________ to get her before she (4. reach) __________ the road, if it was the last thing he did on earth. But he was too late. He saw Jessica (5. run) __________ onto the road. Suddenly a car (6. come) __________ round a bend.

Jessica ran right into it. She went flying through the air. He could not help feeling *thrilled*.
There is no way she can have survived that, he thought.
Jessica's body lay motionless on the ground. Two people got out of their car, *panic-stricken*. Mr Lockwood was pretty sure the girl was dead. He looked down at his clothes, which were very dirty. He would have to wash them like he did the night after he had killed Martin. Only this time, nobody would disturb him as Jessica had done the last time. He turned around and slowly walked home.

! ÜBUNG 76

Übung 76: Setzen Sie ein: ***do*** *oder* ***make****?*

1. Mr Lockwood's attempt to kill Jessica is going to __________ things worse.
2. Sergeant Wood had to __________ some research.
3. Michael Logan said he did not __________ anything.
4. Miss Elliot asked Inspector Hudson to __________ her a cup of tea.

5. Miss Anderson wanted Mr Smith to ________ her happy.

6. Jessica had to ________ a lot of running.

The next morning, Mrs Lockwood was standing in the kitchen, making the children's breakfast. Suddenly, she saw Kevin walk by. To her surprise, he was still in his pyjamas.
"Why are you not dressed, young man?" she asked. "And where is Jessica?"
Kevin *shrugged*. He was never in the best of moods in the mornings.
That's the second time she's *slept in*! she thought, a little annoyed. Do I have to do everything myself around here?
Mrs Lockwood went upstairs and knocked on Jessica's door. There was no answer. She knocked again: still no answer. Mrs Lockwood carefully opened the door. To her surprise, Jessica was not in her room. She closed the door again.
"Jessica!" she called.

Übung 77: Haben die Wörter dieselbe Bedeutung? Markieren Sie: richtig ✔ oder falsch – !

ÜBUNG 77

1. relieved/glad ☐
2. outrage/infuriate ☐
3. hinder/help ☐
4. disappeared/missing ☐
5. corner/bend ☐
6. Miss/Ms ☐
7. hand/give ☐
8. slowly/quickly ☐

Again there was no answer. Mrs Lockwood searched the whole house. Her au pair was nowhere to be found. She looked at her watch. Mrs Lockwood had an important *appointment* with a publisher at 10:00. She would never make it if she had to dress the kids and drive them to school! Mrs Lockwood *bumped* into her husband as he came out of his *study*.

"Have you seen Jessica?" she asked.

"No, why, is she not getting the children ready for school?" he asked.

"No, I can't find her anywhere!" Mrs Lockwood explained.

"Maybe she's gone out for a run," Mr Lockwood said.

"A run, I should hope not! Jessica should be getting the children ready. I told her yesterday evening that I had an important interview today."

"Interview?"

"Yes, with a publisher."

"Oh yes, I remember," Mr Lockwood said. "Look, why don't you get ready and I'll take care of the children. It's no problem at all."

"Would you? That would be great!" exclaimed Mrs Lockwood *relieved.*

! ÜBUNG 78

Übung 78: Unterstreichen Sie die Gegenteile im folgenden Abschnitt!

(1. carried on, 2. fresh, 3. bad, 4. hateful, 5. walk, 6. strongly, 7. late)

Then she paused. For the first time she looked at her husband properly. He was looking *pale* and worn.

"Are you all right?" she asked.

"Yes, I'm fine. Just a little overworked, that's all."
Mrs Lockwood gave her husband a *compassionate* look.
"If you're not well, I can…" she started to say.
"No, its fine, darling. Just run along," Mr Lockwood insisted.
She *pinched* his cheek lovingly. He smiled back at her *weakly*. Then Mrs Lockwood hurried towards the stairs. On her way, she turned around.
"And if Jessica turns up in the meantime, tell her I'm very *disappointed* in her. I've got a good mind to send her home early. *Letting me down* like that!"
Mr Lockwood did not react. He just watched his wife hurry up the stairs.

Chapter 9: A Malicious Plan

Mr Lockwood was sitting at his new desk in the bank. He was surfing the internet. He logged into the Google News site and wrote: "Young girl/car crash/moor". He found nothing. Mr Lockwood clenched his fist.
I'm sure she is dead, but I have to know for sure, he thought.
Mr Lockwood's secretary knocked on his door. Mr Lockwood jumped. His nerves *were* not *in a* very *good state*. The secretary entered. Her name was Miss Grahams. Since Olivia Anderson was in jail, Mr Lockwood had had to get a *replacement* for her.
"Inspector Hudson and Miss Elliot are here to see you," Miss Grahams said.
"To see me? Why?" Mr Lockwood asked, a little too anxiously.
Miss Grahams was *mystified* by his strange behaviour.
"They have an *appointment*, John," she stated.
"Oh yes, of course," he said, almost *apologising*.

ÜBUNG 79

Übung 79: Vervollständigen Sie die Sätze mit dem richtigen Adjektiv!
(difficult, happy, afraid, helpful, anxious, wicked, angry, lazy)

1. A person who kills is ______________.

2. A person who laughs is ______________.

3. A person who fears is ______________.

4. A person who yells is ______________.

5. A person who is nervous is ______________.

6. A person who likes to give someone a hand is ______________.

7. A murder case that is hard to solve is ______________.

8. A person who always gets up late is ______________.

Miss Elliot and Inspector Hudson entered the room. They greeted Mr Lockwood and shook his hand.
"Please take a seat," Mr Lockwood said.
The investigators sat down.

ÜBUNG 80

Übung 80: Ordnen Sie die Begriffe einander zu!

1. ☐ enter	a) thought
2. ☐ shake	b) appointment
3. ☐ brain	c) water
4. ☐ calendar	d) door
5. ☐ flood	e) hand
6. ☐ knock	f) room

7. ☐ search g) find
8. ☐ money h) bank

"I'm so glad you could come," Mr Lockwood *carried on*. "If the press hears about the missing money, there will be a great outcry. Is there a connection between Martin's murder and the *embezzled* money?"
"We're not quite sure yet," answered Miss Elliot. "However, it looks like Martin Smith took the money. We *traced* the transactions *back* to his PC."
"Good Lord!" exclaimed Mr Lockwood, playing his role well. "Martin… a… thief? Never in my dreams would I have thought him *capable* of such a thing!"

Übung 81: Welche Synonyme gehören zusammen? Ordnen Sie zu!

!
ÜBUNG 81

1. ☐ ring a) belongings
2. ☐ things b) God
3. ☐ dream c) communicate
4. ☐ Lord d) frank
5. ☐ express e) delusion
6. ☐ sincere f) call
7. ☐ pretty g) beautiful

"Yes, he didn't do a very good job of clearing up the *trace*s in the system," added Inspector Hudson. "What puzzles us, though, is that he had no true motivation. Did Mr Smith mention anything to you about having money problems?"
"No," Mr Lockwood answered. "And if he did, I'm not sure he would have said anything. We weren't that close."

"Why not?" the inspector inquired. Anyway, you knew about his affair."

"Well, I mean, erm, it just wasn't his style to talk about money."

"I see," remarked Inspector Hudson. "You're absolutely sure you know nothing about it?"

"Yes," replied Mr Lockwood, as *sincerely* as he could.

Mr Lockwood turned to Elvira Elliot.

"Miss Elliot, have you been able to *trace* where the money was transferred to?" he asked.

"No, I'm afraid not. You wanted to give me some new data. That might help," she replied.

"Oh yes, I'll get Miss Grahams to see to that as soon as possible."

"The sooner the better," Miss Elliot said charmingly, but not without *urgency*.

Mr Lockwood's phone rang. He excused himself and picked up the *receiver*.

"Hello...Yes, I know, darling, it's not usually like her...What? You don't think she had her shoes on...? But dear, I'm sure there is some

kind of *explanation*... Okay... I will... Goodbye!"

"Anything wrong?" asked Inspector Hudson, as Mr Lockwood *hung up*.

"Our au pair has gone missing and we've no idea where she is."

"Miss Langer?" the inspector inquired.

"Yes," answered Mr Lockwood.

"She's just *disappeared*?" Inspector Hudson asked, with a note of surprise in his voice.

"I guess she was maybe out late and slept at a friends or something," said Mr Lockwood.

"She didn't seem like the *unreliable* type to me," stated Inspector Hudson.

Übung 82: Welche Wörter gehören in die Lücken?
(ago, during, last)

1. The policemen visited Mr Lockwood ________ his working hours.

2. ___________ night Jessica disappeared.

3. Elvira Elliot had already heard about the embezzlement ___________ Monday.

4. It was a while ___________ that something so dreadful had happened.

5. Mr Lockwood was much happier two weeks ___________.

6. ___________ the questioning Sergant Wood found out that Miss Anderson left work shortly after Mr Smith.

7. Miss Anderson wanted to leave Michael Logan long ___________.

"Well, you can't look inside their heads, can you," said Mr Lockwood with a smile.
"You certainly can't," agreed Miss Elliot.
"I'm sure she'll turn up," said Mr Lockwood.
He looked at his watch.
"Oh, I have a conference call in two minutes, if you would please excuse me."
They all shook hands.
"I'll get my secretary to get those missing *files* to you as soon as possible," Mr Lockwood said.
Inspector Hudson and Elvira Elliot said goodbye and left the bank.

! ÜBUNG 83

Übung 83: Unterstreichen Sie das im Kontext passende Wort!

"Mr Lockwood seemed not quite (1.) herself/himself today, don't you think?" Elvira Elliot said to Inspector Hudson as they (2.) dived/walked along the street.

"Yes, he appeared, how may I say, a little (3.) *bumpy*/*jumpy*."

"I (4.) wander/wonder what was wrong with him. He was supposed to give me the missing data yesterday and he's still not got his act together," Elvira Elliot said.

"Perhaps it's all getting (5.) to/too much for him. His boss being killed, the missing money, an employee charged with murder…" Inspector Hudson said.

"Talking about Olivia Anderson, (6.) have/has she *admitted* to the murder?"

"No, she's *been consigned* to the jail's (7.) medical/torture department. For two days she has neither spoken nor eaten."

"That's awful!" remarked Miss Elliot.

"We've not been able to question her about the money."

"Once Mr Lockwood gets me those missing *files*, we might gain more clarity," Elvira Elliot answered.

"I hope Miss Langer is okay," said Inspector Hudson.

"Miss Langer?" asked Elvira Elliot.

"Mr Lockwood's au pair, very nice girl. And very *keen on* helping me *solve* the murder case," the inspector replied.

They walked past a *fancy* modern coffee shop.

"Care for some coffee, Inspector?" Miss Elliot asked.

"Do they also do tea?" Inspector Hudson inquired sceptically.

"Yes, of course they do!" laughed Miss Elliot. "My treat", she said smiling.

The two investigators walked into the coffee shop.

Übung 84: Füllen Sie die Lücken mit ***do*** *oder* ***does****!*

ÜBUNG 84 !

1. ______ Inspector Hudson really not like coffee?
2. ______ Elvira Elliot drive fast?
3. ______ I know you?
4. ______ Inspector Hudson have a suspect?
5. How ______ you ______?
6. Where ______ Mrs Lockwood stay?
7. Why ______ the inspector think Mr Smith didn't embezzle the money on his own?

It was early in the evening and Jessica had still not turned up. Mrs Lockwood was getting worried. The kids kept on asking her every ten minutes where Jessica was. This just made the worrying worse. Mrs Lockwood asked her husband to take the children to the cinema. She wanted to stay at home in case Jessica eventually turned up. Mr Lockwood and the kids were just about to walk out of the door when the telephone rang.
"Could you get it, dear, I was just going to dry my hair," Mrs Lockwood called from upstairs.

Übung 85: Welcher Satz enthält die richtige Zeitform? Kreuzen Sie an!

ÜBUNG 85 !

1. Inspector Hudson setzte sich hin.
   a) ☐ Inspector Hudson had sat down.
   b) ☐ Inspector Hudson sits down.

c) ☐ Inspector Hudson sat down.

2. Ich werde mich später mit ihr in Verbindung setzen.
   a) ☐ I will get in touch with her later.
   b) ☐ I will be getting in touch with her later.
   c) ☐ I was going to get in touch with her later.

3. Früher war Mr Lockwood einfacher Bankangestellter.
   a) ☐ Mr Lockwood was going to the bank early.
   b) ☐ Mr Lockwood used to be a normal bank employee.
   c) ☐ Mr Lockwood went to the bank early.

4. Inspector Hudson starrte gerade nachdenklich aus dem Fenster.
   a) ☐ Inspector Hudson stares thoughtfully out of the window.
   b) ☐ Inspector Hudson was staring thoughtfully out of the window.
   c) ☐ Inspector Hudson stared thoughtfully out of the window.

5. Sergeant Wood hat schon geholfen viele Fälle zu lösen.
   a) ☐ Sergeant Wood has helped solve many cases.
   b) ☐ Sergeant Wood helped solve many cases.
   c) ☐ Sergeant Wood helps solve many cases.

Mr Lockwood told his children to wait a second and answered the phone.
"Hello… Yes… Oh God, that's terrible… When did this happen?... Yes… I see…"
Mr Lockwood slowly put the phone back down. He was as *pale* as the white, deadly moon which had shone down on his terrible crime the night before. Mrs Lockwood popped her head over the *banister*. She saw her husband's face.

"John, what's wrong?" Mrs Lockwood asked worriedly.
"It's Jessica… She's been in a car accident… She's… She's in a coma," he answered.
"Oh my God, in a coma?!"
Mrs Lockwood came down the stairs.
"How did it happen?" she asked.
"I'm not quite sure. It was last night out near the moors, she ran into a car."
"But how could that happen?"
"I don't know. Maybe she was out jogging."
"Jogging?!" Mrs Lockwood said, perplexed. "Then it must have been after midnight, because that was the last time I saw her. In which hospital is she?"
"St. Anna's," Mr Lockwood answered.
"Okay, I'll go there right away. You take the children to the neighbours and then we'll meet at the hospital."
"Meet at the hospital?" Mr Lockwood replied in an *insecure* voice.
"Yes," replied Mrs Lockwood. "And contact her parents in Germany…"
Mrs Lockwood bit her lip. She was close to tears.
"I hope to God that she recovers," her voice *trembled*.
Mr Lockwood *hugged* his wife.

Übung 86: Schreiben Sie die Zahlen aus!

1. 0 ______________

2. 20 ______________

3. 30 ______________

4. 40 ______________

! ÜBUNG 86

5. 50 ____________

6. 60 ____________

7. 70 ____________

Barbara and Kevin came running from the front door.
"Mummy, Daddy, is everything all right?" they asked.
Mr Lockwood turned to them.
"I'm afraid not," he replied.
His voice sounded *grave* and tired.
If Jessica wakes out of the comma, I'm in big trouble. I have to do something fast! he thought, while he looked into the worried faces of his *beloved* children.

! ÜBUNG 87

*Übung 87: Vervollständigen Sie die Sätze mit **anywhere, nobody, anybody, nothing, anything**!*

1. Michael Logan claimed he had ____________ to do with the murder.
2. Miss Anderson has not said ____________ that could prove her innocence.
3. Michael Logan was not ____________ near the Moor at the time of the Murder.
4. Miss Elliot does not really like ____________ driving her car.
5. On the day of Mr Smith's murder, there were a few people out on the moors. You couldn't say there was ____________ out there.

Inspector Hudson put the phone down. He had just been talking to Mrs Lockwood and heard all about Jessica's *fate*. He sighed.
That poor girl, whatever was she doing out on the moors at that time of night? the inspector thought.
Suddenly his phone rang again. It was Elvira Elliot.
"I've got some news," she said.
"What?" Inspector Hudson asked.
"I've *discovered* something interesting concerning the transaction data…"
Elvira Elliot paused.

Übung 88: Ergänzen Sie die Sätze mit dem passenden "question tag"!

1. Sergeant Wood would never drive a red sports car, *would he?*
2. Jessica would always help Inspector Hudson, __________?
3. Mr Smith was a very hard-working man, __________?
4. Mr Lockwood is not a very nice man, __________?
5. Elvira Elliot is very attractive, __________?
6. Inspector Hudson sure does like to solve crimes, __________?
7. Jessica was in a terrible accident, __________?

"Quit the suspense, it's not a crime show we're on," the inspector said, urging her to continue.
"It looks like Martin Smith didn't *embezzle* the money."
"What?"
"Yes," said Elvira Elliot enjoying *keeping the inspector on tenter-*

hooks. "There was one minor transaction a day after his death."
"Are you sure? How did you find this out?"
"Well, whoever did it tried to cover it up…"
"Do you think Miss Anderson tried to get some more money?"
"Good question, but I doubt it. To pull this kind of thing off you need specialised financial knowledge, which I doubt she has."
"Do you think it was Lockwood?" asked the inspector.
"It's just a guess at the moment. But I got my connections going and also found out that he gambled a lot. He *owes* someone a lot of money."
"Who does he *owe* the money?"
"Can't tell you, client's secret, if you know what I mean. But believe me, it's a lot of money…"
Suddenly Miss Elliot's mobile beeped and she was gone. Inspector Hudson tried to call her back, but he only got her voicemail.
"Perhaps her battery is empty," Inspector Hudson said to himself. She would probably call back soon.

ÜBUNG 89 !

Übung 89: Finden Sie das passende Synonym und ordnen Sie zu!

1. ☐	fate	a) shiver
2. ☐	tremble	b) bet
3. ☐	secret	c) small
4. ☐	tell	d) novel
5. ☐	want	e) anticipation
6. ☐	client	f) destiny
7. ☐	gamble	g) mystery
8. ☐	book	h) customer
9. ☐	minor	i) desire
10. ☐	suspense	j) inform

He sat back and started to think about the case. Inspector Hudson found it strange that Jessica had been running through the moors in the middle of the night without her shoes on. And the people from the car which had *knocked her down* had said that she appeared to be frightened and running away from something. What had really happened that night? His thoughts wandered. The inspector remembered Jessica telling him about the argument between Mr Smith and Mr Lockwood. And if Mr Lockwood had stolen the money, there might be a connection. Inspector Hudson picked up the phone. It rang twice and then Sergeant Wood answered.

"Inspector?" he said.

"I was wondering about that mobile phone. Have we been able to get it working again?" Inspector Hudson asked.

"I haven't heard anything yet. I'll contact the laboratory and call you straight back."

Inspector Hudson put the phone back down.

Übung 90: Wählen Sie die richtige Variante aus!

1. Elvira Elliot spoke __________.

a) ☐ warm   b) ☐ warmly

2. Mr Lockwood tried to answer __________.

a) ☐ calm   b) ☐ calmly

3. Martin Smith was __________ killed.

a) ☐ violently   b) ☐ violent

4. Mr Lockwood spoke in a __________ tone.

a) ☐ harshly   b) ☐ harsh

5. Olivia Anderson was in __________ trouble.

a) ☐ much b) ☐ a lot of

6. Inspector Hudson was __________ prepared.

a) ☐ good b) ☐ well

7. The whole crime couldn't really get any __________.

a) ☐ badder b) ☐ worse

Mr and Mrs Lockwood sat silently beside Jessica's bed in the hospital. She *was* not *in a* very *good state*. Her face was blue and *bruised* and her head was bandaged. There were *tubes* everywhere. In the background you could hear the *uncanny* beeping noise of the life-support machine. Suddenly Mrs Lockwood's mobile phone rang. It was the neighbours saying that the children were crying for their Mum and would not stop. She said she would come immediately. Mrs Lockwood put her coat on.

! ÜBUNG 91

*Übung 91: Setzen Sie richtig ein: **few** oder **little**?*

1. A _____ patients wandered around the hospital.
2. There's _____ chance of Jessica being able to escape from Mr Lockwood.
3. _____ people know what Mr Lockwood is really like.
4. Inspector Hudson just needs a _____ days to solve the case.
5. Sergeant Wood likes a _____ milk with his tea.
6. Inspector Hudson had only a _____ questions.

"I'll stay on a little, if you don't mind," said Mr Lockwood. "Maybe she'll come to and will be happy to see a familiar face."
Mrs Lockwood smiled at her husband.
"That's very kind of you," she said.
Mrs Lockwood kissed her husband lovingly and left the room. Mr Lockwood walked to the door. He looked out to see if *the coast was clear*. In the distance he could see a nurse, but she was busy talking to a doctor. Mr Lockwood closed the door again and walked into the room. He looked at Jessica. She lay helpless in her bed – *oblivious* to the fact that she was about to be murdered.

Übung 92: Wie lautet das Wort auf Englisch?

1. unschuldig ______________
2. neugierig ______________
3. Mut ______________
4. zwicken ______________
5. Spuren ______________
6. Gewehr ______________
7. dringend ______________

Inspector Hudson and Sergeant Wood were sitting in a car on their way to the Lockwoods' house.
"How could we have let ourselves be so *fooled*?" Inspector Hudson exclaimed. "If we hadn't been able to restore the text message from Mr Lockwood to Mr Smith saying that they were to meet on the moors, he might have got away with it!"

"Yes, it's *amazing* what modern technology can do," said Sergeant Wood.
"Yes, yes," replied Inspector Hudson with a note of impatience in his voice.
Sergeant Wood stopped the car in front of the Lockwoods' house. They got out.
"I also talked to Miss Elliot earlier and it looks like Mr Lockwood also took the money from the bank," said Inspector Hudson.
"Do you think Martin Smith found out and that's why he was killed?" asked the sergeant.
"Exactly!" replied Inspector Hudson. "It also appears to be that Mr Lockwood had lost a large *amount* of money gambling."
Inspector Hudson looked at the house and then pointed at it.
"If Miss Elliot *is* not *mistaken*, this does actually not belong to him anymore."

ÜBUNG 93 !

*Übung 93: Vervollständigen Sie die Sätze mit **after** oder **before**!*

1. ____________ about 60 minutes Mrs Lockwood left the hospital.
2. ____________ she left she kissed her husband goodbye.
3. ____________ Mrs Lockwood left, Mr Lockwood closed the door.
4. A short time passed ____________ he decided how to kill Jessica.
5. ____________ Jessica knew it she would be dead.
6. The police will hopefully arrive ____________ he can complete his wicked plan.

Sergeant Wood rang the Lockwoods' doorbell. Mrs Lockwood opened the door. She was surprised to see the policemen at this time of night.
"Is your husband at home?" asked Inspector Hudson.
"No, he's at the hospital with Jessica," she answered.
As soon as Inspector Hudson heard this, he ran to the car. Sergeant Wood and Mrs Lockwood *were* slightly *taken aback by* this sudden action. Sergeant Wood said goodbye to Mrs Lockwood and also hurried towards the car.
"Jessica is in great danger!" exclaimed the inspector as he got back into the car. "I should have listened to her in the first place!"
Sergeant Wood put the siren on and drove away fast.

Übung 94: Wie lauten die Sätze in der richtigen Reihenfolge?

ÜBUNG 94 !

1. appears Mr Lockwood a of that it lost money had amount great

2. the told text message policemen the moors the that they at had met

3. great Jessica is danger in

4. siren Wood put Sergeant on the

5. belong house not Miss if does the was anymore Elliot him mistaken to not

6. was kill Mr to going Lockwood Jessica

7. technology modern can amazing what it's do

Mr Lockwood was still looking at Jessica. He was *hesitant*. Deep in his heart he was not a cold blooded murderer… How would he do it? He could *suffocate* her with a pillow.

It's much easier to shoot someone than kill them with your bare hands, he thought.

He could also pull out some of the cables from the life-supporting machine, but that might set the alarm off. Mr Lockwood picked up a pillow from an empty bed and slowly walked over to her.

ÜBUNG 95 !

Übung 95: Bilden Sie Sätze mit dem Komparativ!

1. Mrs Smith/Inspector Hudson (rich)

Mrs Smith is richer than Inspector Hudson.

2. bank building/Lions Arms (tall)

3. Inspector Hudson/Sergeant Wood (short)

4. Miss Elliot's car/Sergeant Wood's car (expensive)

5. Inspector Hudson/Jessica (old)

6. the weather in London/the weather in Berlin (bad)

Sergeant Wood *sped* around a corner. Inspector Hudson held on to the *dashboard*. Normally he would not tolerate such driving. However, this was a matter of life and death. The car came to a dramatic halt in front of the hospital. The policemen hurried out of the car and ran towards the entrance. They entered the building, causing a lot of *commotion*. What are the police doing here? the faces of the people seemed to say.

Übung 96: Welche der folgenden Aussagen sind wahr? Markieren Sie mit richtig ✔ oder falsch – !

ÜBUNG 96 !

1. Mr Lockwood and Mr Smith were friends. ☐
2. Jessica found Mr Smith's body. ☐
3. Mr Smith had many enemies. ☐
4. Inspector Hudson knows Mrs Lockwood's novel. ☐
5. Sergeant Wood dislikes Elvira Elliot. ☐
6. Mr Smith had an affair with Miss Graham. ☐
7. Inspector Hudson likes fast driving. ☐

Just as Mr Lockwood was about to place the pillow onto Jessica's face, her eyes flickered slightly. Mr Lockwood froze. Jessica was gradually coming to. Suddenly she saw Mr Lockwood. The electro diagram on the *ECG* monitor started to move hectically. Jessica could not scream because she had a *tube* in her mouth. There was a loud, *piercing tone* coming from the monitor *speakers*. This did the screaming for her. Mr Lockwood placed the pillow on Jessica's face and pressed it down with all his might. Jessica's body *twitched* and turned, but she did not have the strength to fight him off. Mr Lockwood was sweating. The twitching was getting less. The line on the *ECG* monitor was getting straighter and the beeping noise was getting more *consistent*. Suddenly the hospital room door flew open and the policemen came running in, followed by a doctor and two nurses. Sergeant Wood *tore* Mr Lockwood *away* from Jessica and threw him to the ground. Mr Lockwood lay there and did not move. The nurses and the doctors hurried over to Jessica. Her heart had stopped. They started to reanimate her. Inspector Hudson watched in horror.

ÜBUNG 97

Übung 97: Welche Verben und Substantive gehören zusammen?

1. ☐ make	a) a steak
2. ☐ knock	b) a fuss
3. ☐ commit	c) an interview
4. ☐ eat	d) a crime
5. ☐ conduct	e) at the door
6. ☐ solve	f) a rifle
7. ☐ fire	g) a case

If Jessica dies, it's my fault. I should have taken her more seriously! he thought.

Then all of a sudden her heart started to beat again. Jessica opened her eyes.

"Thank God!" Inspector Hudson said, his lips moving silently.

The doctor started to give her *oxygen*. Jessica's head turned slightly in the direction of the inspector. A weak smile appeared upon her face. Sergeant Hudson *picked* Mr Lockwood *up* and put *handcuffs* on him. He let himself be led out of the hospital room without any struggle.

"Is she going to be okay?" Inspector Hudson asked.

"I think so," replied the doctor. "But only time can really tell."

Inspector Hudson gave him his business card.

"Please contact me as soon as she is fit enough for visitors," Inspector Hudson said.

The doctor took the card and said he would contact him as soon as Jessica had recovered.

Übung 98: Fügen Sie die Übersetzung der angegebenen Wörter ein!

After eight (1. Wochen) __________ Jessica was fit enough to fly home. Inspector Hudson *picked* her *up* from the hospital and drove her to the airport. He (2. begleitete) __________ her to the gate.

"Thank you once more, Inspector Hudson. You saved my (3. Leben) __________," Jessica said.

Inspector Hudson shook his head.

"I should have listened to you (4. früher) __________ and all of that would never have happened. Mr Lockwood had everything very well planned. I was so (5. sicher) __________ that we had *solved* the case, when we arrested Miss Anderson."

"Well, it's over now," said Jessica. "Why (6. genau) __________ did Mr Lockwood kill Mr Smith?"

"It appears to be that Mr Smith found out about the *embezzlement* and tried to (7. überreden) __________ him to give the money back. As a friend, he wanted to give Mr Lockwood a second chance. And as we know, that turned out to be a fatal (8. Fehler) __________."

Jessica put her arms around the inspector. He was slightly irritated by this gesture and *hugged* her back *awkwardly*.
"Now you take care," he said.
Jessica *nodded*. Inspector Hudson took something out of his pocket and handed it to her. Jessica took it and turned it in her hand. It was an old Scotland Yard police badge.
"It belonged to my Grandfather, I would like you to have it," Inspector Hudson said.
"But Inspector, I can't accept this," Jessica replied.
"No, no, please take it."
Jessica smiled.
"Thank you very much!" she said.

! ÜBUNG 99

Übung 99: Schreiben Sie diese Zahl aus, als würden Sie eine Telefonnummer sprechen!

030 6789 730 __________

To Inspector Hudson's surprise, she gave him a quick kiss on the cheek and walked towards the departure gate. When she got there,

Jessica turned around and *waved*. Inspector Hudson *waved* back. I'm going to miss that girl, he thought.
"Now don't start crying," said a voice behind him.
It was Elvira Elliot and beside her stood Sergeant Wood. They *waved*, too. Jessica *waved* back.
"What are you two doing here?" the inspector asked.
"Observing the sentimental side of Inspector Hudson," Elvira Elliot said with a smile. "Something we would be pleased to see a little more often."
Sergeant Wood *smirked*. Inspector Hudson gave him a warning look. Then he looked towards the gate again. Jessica was walking through passport control.

Übung 100: Welche dieser englischen Begriffe assoziiert man mit Moor? Kreuzen Sie an!

! ÜBUNG 100

1. bog ☐
2. swamp ☐
3. ocean ☐
4. highland ☐
5. marsh ☐
6. fen ☐
7. damp ☐

Inspector Hudson *waved* for the last time. Then he turned around again.
"All right, back to work!" he announced, and started walking towards the exit.
Sergeant Wood and Elvira Elliot looked at each other, smiled and walked towards the exit, too.

Abschlusstest

Übung 1: Welche Synonyme gehören zusammen? Ordnen Sie zu!

1. ☐ shoot	a) sulky
2. ☐ choose	b) guest
3. ☐ resentful	c) things
4. ☐ peculiar	d) strange
5. ☐ visitor	e) fire
6. ☐ belongings	f) call
7. ☐ ring	g) pick

Übung 2: Wie lauten die Begriffe für Wetterphänomene? Ordnen Sie die Buchstaben zu einem sinnvollen Wort!

1. gigitenhnl ____________
2. imts ____________
3. osilsthnea ____________
4. nnrtehro sihgtl ____________
5. trudneh ____________
6. airn ____________

Übung 3: Welcher Satz enthält die richtige Übersetzung?

1. Ich werde mit Ihnen später über alles reden.
   a) ☐ I will talk to you about everything later.

b) ☐ I was going to talk to you about everything later.

2. Steckte auch Miss Anderson hinter dem Mord?
   a) ☐ Was Miss Anderson part of the murder scheme to?
   b) ☐ Was Miss Anderson part of the murder scheme too?

3. Das Auto gehörte ihr.
   a) ☐ The car belonged to her.
   b) ☐ The car belonged to herself.

4. Mr Lockwood ist immer sehr gut angezogen.
   a) ☐ Mr Lockwood is always very good dressed.
   b) ☐ Mr Lockwood is always very well dressed.

5. Michael Logan war nicht zu Hause.
   a) ☐ Michael Logan was not in home.
   b) ☐ Michael Logan was not at home.

Übung 4: Fügen Sie die richtigen Präpositionen ein!
(in, near, over, at, under, on)

1. Mr Lockwood worked ______ a bank.

2. Jessica hid ______ the table.

3. Mr Smith's body was lying ______ the ground.

4. The rifle was found ______ the lake.

5. Inspector Hudson walked ______ to the diver.

6. The murder happened ______ the Lockwoods' house.

Übung 5: Welches Wort ist das „schwarze Schaf“?

1. erratic, incoherent, consistent, irregular
2. dreaming, awake, asleep, snore
3. drag, leave, pull, heave
4. sun, rain, snow, hailstones
5. close, distant, remote, far
6. strong, feeble, muscular, brawny
7. pale, white, ashen, blue

Übung 6: Welche Gegenteile gehören zusammen?

1. ☐ deadly	a) stillness
2. ☐ suspect	b) credit
3. ☐ motion	c) somebody
4. ☐ miss	d) harmless
5. ☐ nobody	e) save
6. ☐ delete	f) hit
7. ☐ debt	g) victim

Übung 7: Setzen Sie das passende Adjektiv bzw. Adverb ein!
(tall, good, eerie, thoughtfully, helpful, cosy, fast)

1. Inspector Hudson did a very ____________ job.

2. The moor was ____________.

3. Sergeant Wood was a ____________ man.

4. Mr Lockwood was very ____________.

5. Inspector Hudson looked out of the window ___________.

6. Miss Elliot drove ___________.

7. The Lockwoods' house is a ___________ place.

Übung 8: Unterstreichen Sie die richtige Variante!

1. Inspector Hudson told/said Sergeant Wood to come with him.
2. Jessica was the same age like/as Inspector Hudson's niece.
3. Kevin is more small/smaller than Jessica.
4. They meeted/met in the moor.
5. Mr Lockwood picked up the receiver/reciever.
6. Sergeant Wood ran before/after the suspect.
7. Mr Smith had much/many employees.

Übung 9: Setzen Sie, wenn nötig, die richtigen Artikel ein!

1. Elvira Elliot was ______ hour late.

2. Mr Smith warned Mr Lockwood many ______ time.

3. Jessica ate ______ apple after dinner.

4. Sergeant Wood has some important ______ news for the inspector.

5. Mr Lockwood was going to ______ jail.

6. Mrs Lockwood sometimes did not like to get out of ______ bed.

7. Jessica was in ______ study.

Übung 10: Fügen Sie die gesuchten Begriffe ein!

1. Another word for misty: ____________.
2. ____________ Mr Lockwood got home, he put his clothes in the washing machine.
3. You can invest in ____________.
4. The opposite of before is: ____________.
5. Jessica, ____________ life was in danger, ran as fast as she could.
6. A house can also be called an ____________.
7. Misuse of funds: ____________.
8. Michael Logan did not have very ____________ time to get away.
9. ____________ is the female equivalent of husband.
10. Jessica was ____________ Germany.

Lösungen

Übung 1: 1. d 2. j 3. h 4. g 5. a 6. i 7. b 8. c 9. f 10. e
Übung 2: 1. mother 2. his 3. consistent 4. bright 5. answer 6. awake 7. decline 8. lips
Übung 3: 1. preferring 2. taking 3. humming 4. running 5. lying 6. travelling 7. dying 8. getting 9. sitting
Übung 4: 1. at school 2. by plane 3. from London 4. on Sunday 5. in the sky 6. in the morning 7. at night 8. on the table 9. In the 21st century 10. at the age of
Übung 5: 1. was 2. got 3. went 4. heard 5. fell 6. came 7. did 8. ate 9. let 10. said
Übung 6: 1. I can't 2. That's 3. I don't 4. you're 5. we'll 6. it's 7. couldn't 8. I'm 9. he's 10. doesn't
Übung 7: 1. half past seven 2. ten past eleven 3. quarter past three 4. midnight 5. quarter to two 6. five to three 7. six minutes past five
Übung 8: 1. early 2. luckily 3. hunter 4. nobody 5. evening 6. share 7. receiver 8. disappointed 9. chatter
Übung 9: 1. leeped (leaped) 2. upstares (upstairs) 3. piked (picked) 4. Amerika (America) 5. ansered (answered) 6. mis (miss)
Übung 10: 1. in 2. over 3. on 4. near 5. under 6. at 7. into
Übung 11: 1. who 2. which 3. what 4. where 5. who 6. whose 7. where
Übung 12: 1. breath 2. behaviour 3. jokes 4. carry on 5. appointment 6. strain
Übung 13: 1. e 2. f 3. a 4. b 5. c 6. d 7. h 8. g
Übung 14: 1. They aren't 2. He isn't 3. We didn't 4. She won't 5. It can't 6. They wouldn't 7. I haven't killed
Übung 15: 1. met/met 2. run/ran 3. say/said 4. made/made 5. keep/kept 6. know/knew 7. thought/thought
Übung 16: 1. alert 2. gracious 3. stunned 4. skinny 5. shock 6. argue 7. blurred 8. tiny 9. fog
Übung 17: 1. slowly 2. thoughtfully 3. fast 4. late 5. safely 6. roughly
Übung 18: 1. sleap (sleep) 2. tosed (tossed) 3. darknes (darkness) 4. incedent (incident) 5. darc (dark) 6. apeared (appeared) 7. downstares (downstairs) 8. kichen (kitchen)
Übung 19: 1. too 2. to 3. too, to 4. too 5. to
Übung 20: 1. i 2. h 3. f 4. e 5. d 6. a 7. b 8. g 9. c 10. j 11. l 12. k
Übung 21: 1. were 2. told 3. at 4. as 5. ran 6. after
Übung 22: 1. Mr Lockwood agreed. 2. There are different kinds of hunting rifles. 3. Mr Smith was acquainted with Mr Lockwood. 4. Inspector Hudson took care

of Miss Anderson. 5. Sergeant Wood followed the suspect.

Übung 23: 1. much 2. much 3. many 4. many 5. much 6. many 7. much

Übung 24: 1. You can buy rifles for hunting foxes, ducks and turkeys. 2. Jessica comes from Germany. 3. Mr Lockwood works at a bank. 4. Miss Anderson's boyfriend is a jealous person. 5. No, she didn't admit to having an affair with him. 6. She could not sleep because Mr Smith's death haunted her. 7. Miss Anderson's boyfriend ran away from the policemen.

Übung 25: 1. richtig 2. falsch 3. richtig 4. falsch 5. falsch 6. falsch 7. falsch

Übung 26: 1. egg 2. assume 3. perhaps 4. leave 5. honest 6. yawn 7. remember 8. voice Lösung: employee

Übung 27: 1. him 2. me 3. his 4. mine 5. her 6. my/his

Übung 28: 1. cloakroom 2. puddle 3. abandoned 4. stick 5. computer 6. scenery 7. pirates

Übung 29: 1. knocked 2. tapped 3. remarked 4. authoritarian 5. ram 6. collapsed

Übung 30: 1. Inspector Hudson would never call on a dangerous criminal without Sergeant Wood. 2. Sergeant Wood would not like to admit that he would not do this, either. 3. Michael Logan would never leave his house with a knife. 4. Inspector Hudson would like to catch the murderer. 5. Michael Logan would like to escape. 6. Sergeant Wood would rather prefer not to have rabies.

Übung 31: 1. myself 2. yourself 3. himself 4. herself 5. ourselves 6. yourselves 7. themselves

Übung 32: 1. took 2. find 3. shrugged 4. said 5. started 6. smiled 7. forced 8. thought

Übung 33: 1. – 2. the 3. a 4. an 5. – 6. the 7. –

Übung 34: 1. His fingerprints were on the weapon. 2. Mr Lockwood wanted to take the phone to the lost property office. 3. Inspector Hudson does not believe Michael Logan. 4. Michael Logan knew about the affair. 5. Sergeant Wood had a bandage around his hand. 6. The suspect is a very jealous man. 7. Michael Logan lured Mr Smith into the moor.

Übung 35: 1. more important/most important 2. stronger/strongest 3. more/most 4. more/most 5. more helpful/most helpful 6. cleverer/cleverest

Übung 36: 1. awake 2. opened 3. small 4. downstairs 5. dislikes 6. working 7. hard

Übung 37: 1. will 2. would 3. would have 4. would 5. will

Übung 38: 1. e 2. g 3. d 4. a 5. f 6. c 7. b

Übung 39: 1. immediately 2. good 3. in 4. under 5. wide 6. followed

Übung 40: 1. ago 2. since 3. ago 4. for 5. since

Übung 41: 1. b 2. b 3. a 4. b 5. b 6. a
Übung 42: 1. good 2. well 3. good 4. good 5. well 6. good 7. well
Übung 43: 1. He felt really dull. 2. Then he threw it out of the window. 3. It clearly belonged to Sergeant Wood. 4. Olivia Anderson spoke to him in his dreams. 5. It looked like the sun might come out.
Übung 44: 1. brutal 2. far 3. good 4. high 5. low 6. straight 7. only
Übung 45: 1. f 2. d 3. a 4. b 5. c 6. g 7. e
Übung 46: 1. secretary 2. mobile 3. rifle 4. commotion 5. insult 6. evidence
Übung 47: 1. hübsch/ziemlich 2. gerecht/nur 3. einzig/nur 4. gesund/gut 5. Hand/geben
Übung 48: 1. lost 2. let 3. paid 4. spent 5. taught 6. wore 7. won 8. shut
Übung 49: 1. Miss Anderson killed him and set him up. 2. Something was not quite right. 3. He was the mysterious phone caller. 4. Perhaps they are in it together. 5. She opened the door fully to let Jessica in. 6. Logan called Mr Smith shortly before his death. 7. Jessica thinks Mr Lockwood is behaving strangely.
Übung 50: 1. Olivia Anderson didn't follow him to the moor. 2. The Lions Arms wasn't near the bank. 3. Inspector Hudson doesn't know who the murderer is. 4. It wasn't very misty. 5. Sergeant Wood's men haven't found a clue.
Übung 51: 1. accompany 2. leave 3. feeble 4. close 5. clear 6. sun 7. time
Übung 52: 1. heart 2. stood 3. tomorrow 4. ourselves 5. went
Übung 53: 1. richtig 2. falsch 3. falsch 4. falsch 5. falsch 6. falsch 7. falsch 8. richtig
Übung 54: 1. room 2. desk 3. lay 4. things 5. pick up 6. flew 7. happily
Übung 55: 1. a 2. a 3. c 4. a 5. b 6. b 7. c
Übung 56: 1. buses 2. planes 3. wishes 4. taxes 5. sandwiches 6. pencils 7. feet 8. fish
Übung 57: 1. will 2. will 3. will 4. going to 5. going to
Übung 58: 1. c 2. h 3. g 4. b 5. d 6. e 7. a 8. f
Übung 59: 1. clever 2. helpful 3. good 4. dangerous 5. funny 6. lucky
Übung 60: 1. handsome 2. stunning 3. attractive 4. gorgeous 5. good-looking 6. pretty
Übung 61: 1. exactly 2. investigate 3. spurned 4. passion 5. evidence 6. inquired
Übung 62: 1. mislay 2. gun 3. wish 4. right 5. guilty 6. doubt 7. normal 8. give
Übung 63: 1. policemen 2. smiles 3. sheep 4. scarves 5. wives 6. halves 7. witnesses 8. ladies 9. teeth
Übung 64: 1. embezzle 2. commotion 3. laboratory 4. funds 5. rocket 6. glad

7. connected 8. coincidence

Übung 65: 1. g 2. e 3. a 4. f 5. c 6. b 7. d

Übung 66: 1. embezzled 2. case 3. accomplice 4. work 5. campaign 6. remain 7. betrayed

Übung 67: 1. through 2. close 3. under 4. to 5. up 6. to 7. up

Übung 68: 1. Jessica was restless. 2. Inspector Hudson wants to talk to Miss Anderson tomorrow. 3. Mr Smith possibly had an accomplice. 4. Jessica had aggravating thoughts. 5. Mr Smith had access to special accounts. 6. It's easier for two people to pull it off. 7. Miss Anderson remains the main suspect.

Übung 69: 1. No, Jessica couldn't sleep. 2. He was carrying a stack of documents. 3. Jessica could not sleep because Mr Smith's death was still bothering her. 4. No, she didn't notice that he was acting strangely. 5. Mrs Lockwood wants to be a novelist. 6. No, she wanted to write him a letter. 7. No, he went straight to his study.

Übung 70: 1. pile 2. amount 3. husband 4. owe 5. Switzerland 6. dizzy 7. lock 8. mistress 9. imprint 10. write 11. dragon 12. account Lösung: embezzlement

Übung 71: 1. Now! 2. Do it right! 3. Stay there! 4. Sit down! 5. Enough of this! 6. Don't do it! 7. Come here! 8. Don't run! 9. Stop it! 10. Not now!

Übung 72: 1. who 2. whose 3. that 4. who 5. which

Übung 73: 1. b 2. c 3. a 4. c 5. a

Übung 74: 1. suspect 2. victim 3. innocent 4. investigation 5. jail/prison

Übung 75: 1. was 2. running 3. had 4. reached 5. run 6. came

Übung 76: 1. make 2. do 3. do 4. make 5. make 6. do

Übung 77: 1. richtig 2. richtig 3. falsch 4. richtig 5. richtig 6. falsch 7. richtig 8. falsch

Übung 78: 1. paused 2. worn 3. fine 4. compassionate 5. run 6. weakly 7. early

Übung 79: 1. wicked 2. happy 3. afraid 4. angry 5. anxious 6. helpful 7. difficult 8. lazy

Übung 80: 1. f 2. e 3. a 4. b 5. c 6. d 7. g 8. h

Übung 81: 1. f 2. a 3. e 4. b 5. c 6. d 7. g

Übung 82: 1. during 2. Last 3. last 4. ago 5. ago 6. During 7. ago

Übung 83: 1. himself 2. walked 3. jumpy 4. wonder 5. too 6. has 7. medical

Übung 84: 1. does 2. does 3. do 4. does 5. do, do 6. does 7. does

Übung 85: 1. c 2. a 3. b 4. b 5. a

Übung 86: 1. zero 2. twenty 3. thirty 4. forty 5. fifty 6. sixty 7. seventy

Übung 87: 1. nothing 2. anything 3. anywhere 4. anybody 5. nobody

Übung 88: 1. would he 2. wouldn't she 3. wasn't he 4. is he 5. isn't she 6. doesn't he 7. wasn't she
Übung 89: 1. f 2. a 3. g 4. j 5. i 6. h 7. b 8. d 9. c 10. e
Übung 90: 1. b 2. b 3. a 4. b 5. b 6. b 7. b
Übung 91: 1. few 2. little 3. few 4. few 5. little 6. few
Übung 92: 1. innocent 2. nosy 3. courage 4. pinch 5. traces 6. rifle 7. urgent
Übung 93: 1. after 2. before 3. after 4. before 5. before 6. before
Übung 94: 1. It appears that Mr Lockwood had lost a great amount of money. 2. The text message told the policemen that they had met at the moors. 3. Jessica is in great danger. 4. Sergeant Wood put the siren on. 5. If Miss Elliot was not mistaken, the house did not belong to him anymore. 6. Mr Lockwood was going to kill Jessica. 7. It's amazing what modern technology can do.
Übung 95: 1. Mrs Smith is richer than Inspector Hudson. 2. The bank building is taller than the Lions Arms. 3. Inspector Hudson is shorter than Sergeant Wood. 4. Miss Eliot's car is more expensive than Sergeant Wood's car. 5. Inspector Hudson is older than Jessica. 6. The weather in London is worse than the weather in Berlin.
Übung 96: 1. richtig 2. falsch 3. falsch 4. falsch 5. falsch 6. falsch 7. falsch
Übung 97: 1. b 2. e 3. d 4. a 5. c 6. g 7. f
Übung 98: 1. weeks 2. accompanied 3. life 4. earlier 5. certain 6. exactly 7. persuade 8. mistake
Übung 99: oh-three-oh six-seven-eight-nine seven-three-oh
Übung 100: 1. bog 2. swamp 5. marsh 6. fen 7. damp

Lösungen Abschlusstest

Übung 1: 1. e 2. g 3. a 4. d 5. b 6. c 7. f
Übung 2: 1. lightening 2. mist 3. hailstones 4. northern lights 5. thunder 6. rain
Übung 3: 1. a 2. b 3. a 4. b 5. b
Übung 4: 1. at 2. under 3. on 4. in 5. over 6. near
Übung 5: 1. consistent 2. awake 3. leave 4. sun 5. close 6. feeble 7. blue
Übung 6: 1. d 2. g 3. a 4. f 5. c 6. e 7. b
Übung 7: 1. good 2. eerie 3. tall 4. helpful 5. thoughtfully 6. fast 7. cosy
Übung 8: 1. told 2. as 3. smaller 4. met 5. receiver 6. after 7. many
Übung 9: 1. an 2. a 3. an 4. kein 5. kein 6. kein 7. the
Übung 10: 1. foggy 2. after 3. funds 4. after 5. whose 6. abode 7. embezzlement 8. much 9. wife 10. from

Glossar

fam	umgangssprachlich
fig	bildlich
pl	Plural
v	Verb

abandon *v*	hier: verlassen; aufgeben
abode	Bleibe
accidentally	versehentlich
add *v* **up**	sich vermehren
admit *v* **sth.**	etwas zugeben
aggravating	ärgerlich
agitated	aufgewühlt
alleged	vermeintlich
amazing	erstaunlich
amount	Summe; Menge
apologise *v*	sich entschuldigen
appointment	Termin
approach *v*	sich nähern
acquainted	(miteinander) bekannt
arrow	Pfeil
as fast as lightening	schnell wie der Blitz
assault and battery	Körperverletzung und Gewaltanwendung
assault	Körperverletzung
astonishment	Erstaunen
awkwardly	unbeholfen; verlegen
banister	Treppengeländer
battering ram	Rammbock
be (was, been) *v* **amongst s.o. things**	in den Sachen von jdm. herumwühlen

be (was, been) *v* **consigned**	übergeben werden
be (was, been) *v* **dressed up**	gut gekleidet sein
be (was, been) *v* **in a good/bad state**	in einem guten/schlechten Zustand sein
be (was, been) *v* **keen on doing sth.**	etwas sehr gerne tun
be (was, been) *v* **mistaken**	sich irren
be (was, been) *v* **oblivious to sth.**	sich einer Sache nicht bewusst sein
be (was, been) *v* **scared**	Angst haben
be (was, been) *v* **taken aback by sth.**	verblüfft sein über etwas
beam *v*	strahlen
bear *v*	ertragen
beg *v* **s.o.**	jdn. anflehen
beloved	geliebt
bewilderedly	verblüfft
bewilderment	Verblüffung
bin	Abfalleimer
boast *v*	angeben
bookshelf, bookshelves *pl*	Bücherregal, Bücherregale
bounce *v* **off**	abprallen
briefly	kurz
brood *v* **over** *fig*	brüten über *fig*
bruised	mit Blutergüssen übersät
brussel sprouts *pl*	Rosenkohl
budge *v*	sich rühren
bulky	sperrig
bullet	Pistolenkugel
bump	Schlag
bump *v*	anstoßen; zusammenstoßen
bumpy	holprig

calm *v* **down**	sich beruhigen
capable	fähig
carry *v* **on with sth.**	mit etwas fortfahren
cartoon	Zeichentrickfilm
casually	beiläufig
chatter *v*	plaudern
cheekiness	Frechheit
cheeky	frech
chuckle *v*	kichern
claim *v*	behaupten
claws *pl*	Krallen
cling *v*	haften
cloakroom	Garderobe
coffee table	Couchtisch
coincidence	Zufall
comb *v*	hier: absuchen, durchkämmen; kämmen
come (came, come) *v* **across sth.**	auf etwas stoßen
commotion	Aufruhr
compare *v*	vergleichen
compassionate	mitfühlend
composed	gelassen
concerned	besorgt
confess *v*	zugeben
confession	Eingeständnis
consistent	gleichmäßig
constable	Polizist
contain *v*	beinhalten
convince *v*	überzeugen
cosy	gemütlich
courage	Mut

creep *v*	hier: aufsteigen; kriechen
cringe *v*	zusammenzucken
crop *v* **up**	auftauchen
cut *v* **in**	hier: ins Wort fallen; einschneiden
cutlery	Besteck
dab *v*	abtupfen
damp	feucht
dashboard	Armaturenbrett
deafening	ohrenbetäubend
deceit	Betrug
deceived	betrogen
deer	Reh
delete *v*	löschen
dense	dicht
deny *v*	abstreiten
descend *v*	hinuntergehen
disappear *v*	verschwinden
disappointed	enttäuscht
disappointment	Enttäuschung
disbelief	Fassungslosigkeit
displeasure	Missfallen
discover *v*	entdecken
dishonest	unehrlich
dismay	Bestürzung
distract *v*	ablenken; verwirren
distrustfully	misstrauisch
divert *v*	umleiten
dizzy	schwindelig
drag *v*	ziehen
dragon	Drache
drawer	Schublade

dump *v* **s.o.** *fam*	jdn. verlassen
ECG	EKG
edge	Kante
eerie	unheimlich
embarrassing	peinlich
embezzlement	Veruntreuung
encourage *v*	ermuntern
erase *v*	löschen
erratic	unregelmäßig
explanation	Erklärung
fairytale	Märchen
fancy	schick
fate	Schicksal
feel (felt, felt) *v* **uneasy**	sich unwohl fühlen
figure *v* **out**	herausfinden
file	Akte; Ordner; Datei
firmly	bestimmt
flashy *fig*	protzig
flick *v* **through**	durchblättern
flimsy	zart
fool *v* **s.o.**	jdn. hereinlegen
forehead	Stirn
frighten *v* **the hell out of s.o.**	jdm. eine Höllenangst einjagen
funds *pl*	Fonds
gasp *v*	hier: Erstaunen zum Ausdruck bringen
gather *v* **(oneself together)**	(sich) zusammennehmen
get (got, got) *v* **to one's feet**	aufstehen
get (got, got) *v* **s.o. wrong**	jdn. falsch verstehen
get (got, got) *v* **a move on** *fam*	sich beeilen
get (got, got) *v* **rid of sth.**	etwas loswerden
giant	riesig

giggle *v*	kichern
give (gave, given) *v* **in**	nachgeben
give (gave, given) *v* **s.o. the creeps**	jdm. nicht geheuer sein
give (gave, given) *v* **s.o. a lift**	jdn. (im Auto) mitnehmen
give (gave, given) *v* **s.o. free rein**	jdm. freie Hand lassen
give (gave, given) *v* **sth. a miss**	auf etwas verzichten
glare *v* **at s.o.**	jdn. zornig anstarren
go (went, gone) *v* **around the bend**	verrückt werden
goblin	Kobold
good mood	gute Laune
grab *v*	greifen
grave	ernst
greasy	fettig
greenish	grünlich
grin	Grinsen
guard *v*	bewachen
guilty	schuldig
guilty conscience	schlechtes Gewissen
handcuffs *pl*	Handschellen
hang (hung, hung) *v* **up**	auflegen
harass *v*	belästigen
harm *v* **s.o.**	jdm. Schaden zufügen
haunt *v*	verfolgen
have (had, had) *v* **a clue**	eine Ahnung haben
have (had, had) *v* **the fright of one's life**	den Schreck seines Lebens haben
hawk	Habicht
head *v* **for**	zusteuern auf
hesitant	zögerlich

hiss *v*	zischen
hollow	Vertiefung
honest	ehrlich
hooded jumper	Kapuzenpulli
horrified	entsetzt
hug *v*	umarmen
hunting season	Jagdsaison
hurt (hurt, hurt) *v* **like mad** *fam*	sehr weh tun
husky	belegt
ill-tempered	schlecht gelaunt
imprint	Abdruck
indeed	in der Tat
ink remover	Tintenkiller
inquisition *fig*	strenges Verhör
insecure	unsicher
instantly	sofort
insulted	beleidigt
interrupt *v*	unterbrechen
intimidated	eingeschüchtert
investigate *v*	ermitteln
it was a shame	es war schade
jagged	spitz
jot *v* **sth. down**	etwas notieren
jumpy *fig*	nervös
keep (kept, kept) *v* **s.o. on tenterhooks**	jdn. auf die Folter spannen
knock *v* **s.o. down**	jdn. überfahren
knowingly	wissend
lab *fam*	Labor
late husband	verstorbener Ehemann
laughter	Gelächter

lead (led, led) *v* **s.o. astray**	jdn. an der Nase herumführen
let (let, let) *v* **s.o. down**	jdn. enttäuschen
liar	Lügner
lock	Türschloss
lose (lost, lost) *v* **one's way**	sich verlaufen
lost for words	sprachlos
lost property office	Fundbüro
lure *v*	locken
make (made, made) *v* **out sth.**	etwas erkennen
make (made, made) *v* **funny faces**	Grimassen schneiden
make (made, made) *v* **s.o. do sth.**	jdn. zu etwas zwingen/bewegen
malfunction	Störung
malicious	arglistig
marksman	Schütze
marshy	sumpfig
match *v*	übereinstimmen
meandering	schlängelnd
mist	Nebel
mistress	Geliebte
misty	neblig
muddy	matschig
mystified	verblüfft
nod *v*	nicken
no doubts *pl*	keine Zweifel
nosy	neugierig
not have (had, had) *v* **the foggiest idea**	nicht die geringste Ahnung haben
not stand *v* **a chance**	keine Chance haben
nursery rhyme book	Kinderliederbuch
obediently	folgsam

obituary	Todesanzeige
obstinate	hartnäckig
occasionally	hin und wieder
odd	merkwürdig
offences *pl*	Vergehen
on a big scale	in großem Umfang
once upon a time ...	es war einmal ...
owe *v*	schulden
oxygen	Sauerstoff
pale	blass
panic-stricken	von Panik erfasst
particularly	besonders
path	Weg
pattern	Muster
peculiar	seltsam
peek *v*	gucken *fam*
persistent	beharrlich
pick *v* **s.o. up**	jdn. abholen/mitnehmen
piercing tone	schriller Ton
pile	Stapel
pin *v* **s.o. down**	jdn. niederhalten
pinch *v*	kneifen
pitch-black	stockdunkel
plead *v*	bitten
poke *v*	stochern; stöbern
police record	Vorstrafen
polite	höflich
pound *v*	hämmern, pochen; stampfen
pounding	Pochen
preoccupied	beschäftigt
press *v* **charges**	Anklage erheben
pretend *v*	so tun als ob, vortäuschen

propose *v* **a toast**	einen Trinkspruch ausbringen
prosecution	Strafverfolgung
puddle	Pfütze
pull *v* **oneself together**	sich zusammenreißen
quarrel *v*	streiten
rabies	Tollwut
rambler	Wanderer
recall *v*	sich erinnern
receive *v*	erhalten
receiver	Telefonhörer
recently	kürzlich
recognise *v*	erkennen
regretfully	bedauernd
relief	Erleichterung
relieved	erleichtert
reluctant	unwillig
replacement	Ersatz
resent *v*	einen Groll hegen
resentful	verärgert
resentment	Groll
restrained	beherrscht
retire *v*	sich zurückziehen
rifle	Gewehr
rightful owner	rechtmäßiger Besitzer
roar *v*	dröhnen
roar *v* **with laughter**	vor Lachen brüllen
rubber	Gummi
run (ran, run) *v* **errands**	Besorgungen machen
scare *v* **the living daylights out of s.o.**	jdn. zu Tode erschrecken
scenery	Landschaft

scramble *v*	klettern
screech *v*	schreien
scribble *v*	kritzeln *fam*
scrutinize *v*	untersuchen, genau ansehen
search warrant	Durchsuchungsbefehl
set (set, set) *v* **s.o. up** *fam*	jdm. die Schuld in die Schuhe schieben
settee	Sofa
sharp	spitz
shelf, shelves *pl*	Regal, Regale
shrug *v*	mit den Achseln zucken
similarity	Ähnlichkeit
sincerely	aufrichtig
skip *v*	hier: auslassen; hüpfen
slamming	zuknallend
slash *v*	hier: mit dem Messer ausholen; aufschlitzen
sleep (slept, slept) *v* **in**	verschlafen
slope	Abhang
smirk *v*	grinsen
snakes and ladders	ein Brettspiel
sneak *v*	schleichen
sob *v*	schluchzen
solve *v*	lösen
sophisticated	anspruchsvoll; elegant
sore	schmerzhaft; schlimm
sorrow	Kummer, Leid
sound *v* **fishy** *fam*	faul klingen
source	Quelle
spare key	Ersatzschlüssel
speakers *pl*	Lautsprecher
speed (sped, sped) *v*	eilen, flitzen *fam*

speeding	Geschwindigkeitsüberschreitung
spit (spat, spat) *v*	hier: fauchen
spit (spat, spat) *v* **fire**	Feuer speien
spot	Stelle
sprain *v*	verstauchen
spread *v* **out**	ausbreiten
spurned love	verschmähte Liebe
spy *v* **on**	hinterherspionieren
stair board	Treppenabsatz
stammer *v*	stottern
steadily	hier: vorsichtig; ununterbrochen
steaming	dampfend
stick	Stock
stir *v*	umrühren; sich rühren
stomach	Bauch
stout	korpulent, kräftig
strain *v*	hier: beanspruchen; anspannen
strain *v* **one's ears**	angestrengt lauschen
stubborn	stur
study	Arbeitszimmer
stunned	verblüfft
suffocate *v*	ersticken
sulky	verdrossen
suspect	Verdächtige(r)
suspicion	Verdacht, Verdächtigung
suspicious	verdächtig
swallow *v*	schlucken
swear *v*	fluchen; schwören
take (took, taken) *v* **a deep breath**	tief Luft holen
tear (tore, torn) *v* **away**	wegreißen

telephone directory	Telefonbuch
the coast is clear *fig*	die Luft ist rein *fig*
threaten *v*	(be)drohen
thrilled	begeistert
throb *v*	pochen
tiptoe *v*	auf Zehenspitzen gehen
toss *v*	sich hin und her wälzen
trace *v* **(back)**	ausfindig machen; jdn. zurückverfolgen
traces *pl*	Spuren
treasure	Schatz
tremble *v*	zittern
tube	Schlauch
tuck *v* **s.o. in**	jdn. zudecken
turkey	Truthahn
tut *v*	Ausdruck des Unbehagens
twist *fig*	überraschende Wendung
twitch *v*	zucken
tyre	Reifen
unbearable	unerträglich
uncanny	unheimlich
unreliable	unzuverlässig
upset *v*	stören
urge	Bedürfnis
urgency	Dringlichkeit
wastepaper basket	Papierkorb
wave *v*	hier: winken; wehen
weakly	hier: schwach; kränklich
wearily	erschöpft
weird *fam*	seltsam
whistle *v*	pfeifen
will	hier: Testament; Wille

windowsill	Fensterbank
wink *v*	zwinkern
witness, witnesses *pl*	Zeuge, Zeugen
worn out	erschöpft
wrap sth. up *fam*	etwas unter Dach und Fach bringen *fig*
wrinkle *v* **one's forehead**	die Stirn runzeln
wrinkle *v* **one's nose**	die Nase rümpfen
yawn *v*	gähnen
Yuck!	Igitt!